HOUND ON THE HEATH

It was chilly in the tent, and Mandy drew up her knees and rolled over, determined to go back to sleep. Then, suddenly, her heart froze.

The chilling sound of a single, high-pitched howl came floating across the moor. She gasped and sat up at the same time as Blackie. Mandy could feel him stiffen, alert and listening.

The sorrowful wail came again and Blackie gave a rumbling growl, while Mandy felt goose bumps break out all over her arms. She'd never heard anything so creepy!

Read more spooky Animal Ark™ Hauntings tales

1 Stallion in the Storm
2 Cat in the Crypt
3 Dog in the Dungeon
4 Colt in the Cave
5 Foal in the Fog
6 Hound on the Heath

Hound
on the
Heath

Ben M. Baglio

Illustrations by Ann Baum

**Cover illustration by
John Butler**

AN
APPLE
PAPERBACK

SCHOLASTIC INC.
New York Toronto London Auckland Sydney
Mexico City New Delhi Hong Kong Buenos Aires

To Hayley with love.

**Special thanks to Ingrid Hoare.
Thanks also to C. J. Hall,
B.Vet.Med., M.R.C.V.S., for reviewing
the veterinary information contained in this book.**

ISBN 0-439-44897-2

12 11 10 9 8 7 6 5 4   3 4 5 6 7/0

Printed in the U.S.A.   40

First Scholastic printing, November 2002

HAUNTINGS

One

"Watch out, Blackie!" Mandy Hope reached out for the collar of the big black Labrador and pulled him toward her. She was perched on a log, facing their small campfire, and sparks from the pyramid of glowing logs were flying in all directions. A pale cloud of ash rose into the air, making Mandy and her friend James Hunter cough.

"Blackie! Stay away from the fire!" James pleaded with his dog. "That's the second time you've used your tail to fan the flames!"

Mandy stroked Blackie's glossy coat, and he settled beside her on the grass, resting his chin on her knee with a big sigh. "He's excited," she said sympathetically.

1

Mandy was as thrilled as Blackie to be spending the school break camping. "You can't blame him. He's not used to spending the night in the middle of the countryside. Isn't it nice?"

James looked over to where Mandy was gazing. Dalton Heath spread as far as they could see in colors of fading green and gold, its heather-covered hills purple in the gathering dusk. Mandy could just make out the steep rise of a craggy cliff face on the horizon. "All it needs is a haunted house and the shriek of the wind on a winter's night and . . ." she began, her voice trembling playfully. She hugged her knees.

"Oh, stop, Mandy." James frowned. "Don't get all spooky on me."

"Hi!" Mandy's father, Dr. Adam Hope, exclaimed as he came striding toward the camp. "I was hoping to catch a whiff of sausages sizzling on the fire by now."

"Mom says they're still frozen solid." Mandy laughed. "She's been searching in the Land Rover to find something else we can cook. Did you find the showers, Dad?"

"Yes," Dr. Adam said cheerfully. "It's quite a hike away and it's not what you might call luxurious — but it's good enough for two intrepid campers like you and James." He grinned at his daughter and her friend, then looked up as his wife appeared. "Hello, sweetie," he said. "What's for supper?"

"Adam," said Dr. Emily Hope, brandishing a pack of sausages, "there were *fresh* sausages for our trip in the fridge at home. You must have taken these from the freezer!" To prove her point, she tapped the sausages on his head.

"Oops!" Dr. Adam shrugged. "Sorry. Can we make do with bacon, eggs, and beans this evening?"

"I suppose we'll have to," Dr. Emily said. "The stores around here will be closed by now." She glanced at her watch. "It's after seven o'clock already!"

"Good," said Mandy, scratching Blackie's ears. "The sooner the night comes, the better, if you ask me."

"Why?" James looked puzzled.

"Because the sooner it will be morning and then we can go off and explore, of course!" Mandy replied.

"It's a shame we got here so much later than planned," Dr. Adam said, looking up at the rapidly darkening sky.

There had been an unavoidable delay before they'd left. Mandy's parents were both veterinarians in the Yorkshire village of Welford, about twenty miles south of Dalton Heath. Drs. Adam and Emily had been hoping to get away from their clinic, Animal Ark, in the early afternoon on the first Friday of the break.

Just as they had been about to leave, a car had come racing into the parking lot and screeched to a stop at the front door. Dr. Adam had immediately dropped everything to perform an emergency operation on a swan that had swallowed a fishhook.

"Well, at least we saved the life of that beautiful bird." Dr. Emily smiled as she rummaged in the cooler for the bacon. "And I'm sure Alistair will take the best possible care of the swan in the clinic," she added.

"Good old Alistair," said Mandy, thinking fondly of the vet who filled in for them when they were away.

"Yes," Dr. Emily agreed as she took eggs and butter out of the cooler.

"You're right," Dr. Adam said, clapping his hands. "Let's get this supper started, OK? James, will you fetch a few more logs before that fire goes out completely? Mandy, can you break some eggs and get them ready for scrambling, please?"

"I'll pour us some drinks," Dr. Emily said with a smile, twisting her long auburn hair into a ponytail clasp.

James returned with his arms laden with firewood left by the previous campers. The fire leaped to life, alarming Blackie, who decided to stay far away. It cracked and fizzled before the flames died down, and Dr. Emily was able to balance the iron frying pan on a neat triangle of logs.

"What a great smell," James said happily. "I'm starving."

In the fierce heat of the fire, a delicious supper was prepared in minutes. Mandy sat cross-legged on the grass beside James and ate heartily. Because she didn't eat meat, Mandy had extra scrambled eggs and beans. A fried banana finished off the meal perfectly.

The setting sun left a stripe of pink in the spring sky, and the trees from the nearby wood began to rustle in a quickening evening breeze. Dr. Emily zipped up her anorak and shivered.

"I've got a guidebook . . . somewhere," said Dr. Adam, groping around in his backpack. "Here it is."

"Can I see, Dad?" Mandy asked. She put her plate on the grass and turned the pages quickly. "Dalton Heath . . . here it is . . . on the eastern edge of the North York Moors."

"There's a river that runs across this part," James piped up. "My dad told me."

"Oh, great!" said Mandy. "We'll have to go and find it tomorrow."

"And there's a market in Dalton that's supposed to be very interesting," Dr. Emily said, collecting the plates. "We need to do some shopping, anyway, and I'd like to browse around a bit."

Mandy looked over at James and wrinkled her nose. She was a little disappointed. She wanted to explore the heath and search for the river with James and Blackie.

Still, it was her mother's vacation, too — and a trip into the town wouldn't hurt.

"OK," she said, and smiled at her mom. "That's all right, isn't it, James?"

"Fine with me." James nodded. "What does it say about Dalton Heath? In the book, I mean."

Mandy lowered her head and squinted at the small print in the glow of the campfire.

"Oooh," she said. "Listen to this! *Visitors who come to explore the beautiful stretch of wilderness that sur-*

*rounds the little town of Dalton are often lured there
by tales of mystery and intrigue. . . ."*

"Oh, Mandy! You're making it up!" James said in disgust.

"I am *not!*" Mandy was indignant. "See for yourself."

James came over and sat beside her. Blackie took the
chance to roll over on to his back, in the hope of having
his tummy tickled. James ignored him, and looked at
the book.

"Continue reading," urged Dr. Adam. "What's the
mystery?"

James took over. *"For as long as anyone can remember, an eerie howling has been heard after dark
from somewhere on the moor. Some locals say that it
is the cry of a mysterious, unknown beast, others that
it is the mournful cry of a dog that died of a broken
heart long ago. . . ."*

Mandy gasped. "Oh! How sad! A broken heart? Why,
what happened?" she asked, reaching for the book.

"It's only a story!" James said, grinning at Mandy's
stricken face.

"Well, read some more!" she insisted.

"No, don't," Dr. Emily said firmly. "It's getting dark,
and we've still got to put up our tents. Come on, let's
not scare ourselves with silly legends that have been
dredged up by the locals to attract tourists. Anyway,

Dad and I were hoping that you two would stay clear of any adventures while we're here."

"Your mom's right." Dr. Adam got to his feet. "We'd better get started if we're going to have somewhere warm and comfortable to sleep tonight. Put the book in the bag, Mandy — and let's forget about it. There'll be time to explore this place for ourselves in the light of a fresh, autumn morning."

Reluctantly, Mandy dropped the book into her father's backpack. She wished that she could find out more, but her parents and James were scurrying around, hauling ground cloths and tent poles out of bags. Mandy put out the fire and then went to help with the tents.

"How about pitching our tent over here?" Dr. Adam suggested, clearing the ground of small stones with his boot. "If Mandy and James decide to talk all night, we won't be disturbed!" He laughed.

"Good idea," Dr. Emily said approvingly, spreading out the ground cloth.

"Let's pitch our tent in this hollow," Mandy said to James. "We'll be protected from the wind by that little hill."

James nodded.

They hammered the tent pegs into the soft, damp earth and, as the tent took shape, Mandy felt her excitement grow. The wild, rolling heather-clad hills and dales

stretched in every direction. The scent from millions of
tiny blossoms was in the air and, to make it all the more
magical, a huge yellow moon was climbing slowly into
the night sky.

Dr. Adam lit three of his portable, oil-burning lamps
and placed them at intervals around the camp.

"It's wonderful!" Mandy exclaimed as she unrolled
their sleeping bags. "It's as if we were the only people
left in the world."

"Leave a space for Blackie to lie between us," said
James. The Labrador was peering in through the tent
flap, looking around expectantly for his basket. James
tossed Mandy a blanket for his dog to sleep on.

"You'll have to make do with that, Blackie," James
said. "There wasn't room for your basket in the Land
Rover."

"Everything OK?" Dr. Adam put his head through the
tent flap.

"Great, Dad," Mandy answered, folding the blanket
for Blackie.

"Get some rest now, you two," said Mandy's dad.
"There are two thousand miles of trails up here."

"Phew!" James said, his eyebrows raised. "We'd need
longer than a few days to do that!"

"What sorts of animals live on the moor?" Mandy
asked.

"Um . . . foxes, badgers, deer, rabbits, that sort of thing," Dr. Adam said.

"There are otters, too," James said importantly. "My dad told me that they live near rivers on the moor. They're quite rare now in this country. He said that we might see ermines, too."

"But did you know that the moors were once covered by huge, prehistoric forests of oak, elm, lime, and yew trees?" said Dr. Adam. "They provided cover for a larger range of animals. But the trees were hacked down by Bronze Age settlers in this area — and the heather took over. Anyway, you can see the moor tomorrow," said Dr. Adam. "Off to bed!"

"Night," Mandy and James chorused together.

The tent was plunged into sudden darkness as Mandy's father turned out the oil lamps standing outside. She listened to his footsteps fade on the stony ground and then, there was silence. Curled up on his blanket, Blackie sighed contentedly.

"It's dark, isn't it?" James whispered after a moment.

"Hmm, quiet, too," Mandy said, adding, "James, did you believe that story about the animal that howls on the moors?"

"I'm not sure," James said cautiously.

"It might be a dog," Mandy suggested. "If it's lost and

living alone on the moor, it would be able to live on rabbits and other creatures."

"But the guidebook said that the howling has gone on for as long as anyone can remember. A dog wouldn't live for that long — it must be something else." James yawned. "Don't worry, I'm sure we won't hear a thing. Anyway, I'm too tired to worry about ghostly howling."

He settled deeper into his sleeping bag, tugging up the zipper so that it all but covered his head. Mandy stretched out a hand to Blackie. The warmth of the big dog's soft coat was comforting. Then she, too, fell asleep.

Two

Mandy woke up suddenly. For a moment, she struggled to think where she was. She lay in the dark, feeling the unfamiliar hardness of the ground underneath her and the cold metal of the sleeping bag's zipper pressing into her chin. Then she remembered. Dalton Heath! Why, she wondered, did she wake up?

The moon had vanished behind thick clouds, and the moor seemed silent and still. Yet Mandy knew that many moorland creatures would be quietly going about their nocturnal business. Beside her, Blackie shuffled and snuffled in his sleep, and James mumbled something about a picnic and gave a little grunt.

It was chilly in the tent, and Mandy drew up her knees and rolled over, determined to go back to sleep. Then, suddenly, her heart froze.

The chilling sound of a single, high-pitched howl came floating across the moor. She gasped and sat up at the same time as Blackie. They were shoulder to shoulder in the two-person tent, and Mandy could feel him stiffen, alert and listening.

The sorrowful wail came again and Blackie gave a rumbling growl, while Mandy felt goose bumps break out all over her arms. She'd never heard anything so creepy.

"James!" she whispered. "James, wake up!"

"Hmm?" murmured James sleepily.

"James!" Mandy's voice was urgent.

"What? What is it?" James yawned noisily. "It's still *dark*, Mandy . . . I was . . ."

"Shh! Listen!" she urged.

The animal out on the moors howled again. It seemed closer this time.

"Owl," said James dismissively, his voice thick with sleep.

"An *owl*? No way! James, are you awake?" Mandy put out a hand and shook her friend.

"Hmm?" James mumbled, then Mandy heard the sleeping bag rustle as he sat up. "What?"

"That's not an owl!" Mandy said.

"It's a fox, then," James said grumpily.

"Or . . ." said Mandy quietly, "perhaps it is a dog after all?" She shook off her sleeping bag and crawled cautiously to the door of the tent. Blackie nudged her aside and pushed his nose out. He was still growling softly.

"Here," said James, "I've got a flashlight. Shine it around and see what's out there." He directed a beam of light at Blackie, who was cheek to cheek with Mandy on her hands and knees in the doorway.

Mandy looked out into the night. There was no sign of the moon, and the moors were a vast expanse of black nothingness. Light from the flashlight cast a pathetic glow on a clump of conifer trees beyond their Land Rover, and little else.

"Well?" James prompted.

Mandy began to shiver. "Nothing," she reported.

"Well, it stopped," James said, yawning again. "Whatever it was, it went back to sleep — which is exactly what we should do."

"Oh, James, what if it *is* a lost dog?" Mandy said worriedly.

"It can't be a dog," James responded. "A lost dog would wander toward the town, where there are people to help it and feed it. It wouldn't roam around up here, alone and hungry, would it? Dogs are sensible animals, they —"

James stopped talking when Blackie attempted to get into his master's sleeping bag. "Out, Blackie!" James said firmly. "Go in your own bed!"

Mandy shined the flashlight on James's irritated face and burst out laughing. "Very sensible!" she said.

"I'm going to sleep," James announced. "If you and Blackie want to go exploring the moors in the middle of the night, you're welcome to."

"Grumpy," Mandy teased, but she climbed back into her sleeping bag, relishing its warmth. For a long time she lay awake, straining her ears for the pitiful sound of the creature's howl. But the moor was silent. Eventually, Blackie's rhythmic breathing soothed Mandy back to sleep.

"Mom's making hot chocolate," Dr. Adam said the next morning, ruffling Mandy's tousled, fair hair as she crawled out of her tent. James appeared behind her, on all fours, and yawned. "You two look as though you didn't sleep a wink!" Dr. Adam chuckled, watching as James stood up and began shuffling toward the camp-fire.

Mandy yawned and rubbed her eyes, wishing now she hadn't spent so much of the night wide awake. She pushed her hair away from her face and smiled at her father.

"So, did you lie awake, whispering for hours?" Dr. Emily smiled as she stirred chocolate powder into a mug of frothy milk.

"Nope," James said, shaking his head. "We didn't talk. We *listened*."

"Listened?" Dr. Emily looked up, frowning.

"Didn't you hear it?" Mandy blurted. "The howling?"

"Aha!" said Dr. Adam, his eyes twinkling. "The brokenhearted dog on the moor. I remember. No, Mandy, we didn't. Did we, Emily?"

"I certainly didn't." Dr. Emily smiled. "I slept very peacefully, thank you."

"Seriously, Dad, we *did* hear it. It was really eerie," Mandy said. "What could it have been? If it wasn't a dog, what was it?"

"Howling? A female fox would be my guess, sweetie." Dr. Adam was slicing some bread. "They make an awful racket when they're out searching for a mate."

"No," said Mandy, shaking her head. "It wasn't a fox. I'm sure of it." Mandy had heard foxes howling from her bedroom window in Welford. The howling she'd heard last night was different.

"Who wants some bread and jam?" Dr. Adam asked, changing the subject. "Isn't it wonderful how the great outdoors gives you such a healthy appetite?"

"Yes," said James with a yawn as he unscrewed

the lid of a jar of raspberry jam and sniffed it. "It's wonderful."

"Blackie heard it, too," Mandy persisted. "He was too scared to leave the tent, but he looked out and growled."

"What a wimp!" Dr. Adam laughed and petted Blackie's head.

"I'm going to brave the communal showers after breakfast," Dr. Emily said. "Then should we explore Dalton?"

Mandy didn't reply. She frowned as she took a bite of her bread. She looked out across the moors. In the crisp light of early morning, it looked serene and beautiful. Yet, somewhere out there, there was a creature in distress. Mandy was sure of it. She couldn't forget the anguished sound of last night.

"Perhaps it was a dream." Dr. Emily spoke quietly, slipping an arm around Mandy's shoulders. "It may just be that, after reading all about the dog in the guidebook, you dreamed about it?"

"But James heard the howling, too!" Mandy reasoned. "I didn't imagine it. I know I didn't." She turned to James, who was sitting astride a log, his cheeks bulging with food. "You heard it, didn't you, James?"

"Sounded like a fox to me," James said, shrugging his shoulders. "Or just an owl, hooting away into the night."

"Oh, James!" said Mandy irritably. "It was *not* a fox or an owl!" She put her mug into the plastic basin. "I'm going to take a shower."

The small town of Dalton was packed with Saturday morning shoppers. The main street had been closed to traffic to allow people to browse safely along a narrow, cobbled road, which led to the large square. Rows of stalls were set out, and merchants shouted about their merchandise to attract customers.

"There's everything from fresh vegetables to fine lace," observed Dr. Adam. "Keep Blackie close to you, James," he added. "We don't want to lose him in this crowd."

Blackie trotted along on his leash, his head high and his nose quivering with interest. There were other dogs on leashes to greet, and the combined enticing smells from the butcher's and baker's stalls kept his tail wagging eagerly.

Dr. Emily paused to admire an antique copper kettle.

"Turkish," said the merchant, who was knitting. "It's real copper. Not fake."

"It's lovely." Dr. Emily smiled, but Mandy saw her mom's eyes widen when she spotted the kettle's price tag. She put it down hastily and moved on to a book stall.

Mandy moved along to a table piled high with edible treats and toys for pets. She chose a rawhide bone for Blackie and searched her jeans pocket for some change.

"Is that your dog?" the merchant asked her. Blackie was sitting obediently at James's feet, with only his shiny black nose visible above the edge of the table.

"No, he belongs to my friend." Mandy smiled.

"He deserves a treat. He's well behaved," the man said. "Not like some."

"Thanks." James grinned and patted Blackie's head.

Mandy accepted her change, then froze as the sound of a long, quavering howl reached her. She widened her eyes, looking at James in amazement. It was almost the same sound that she had heard in the night.

"Oh, you don't want to pay attention to that," the merchant said quickly. "That's Jazz, Mr. Ritchie's dog. He hates to be left, that's all."

"Oh . . ." Mandy was relieved and disappointed all at once. "I thought —"

"He's over there, see?" he interrupted her. "Under the table. Mr. Ritchie went to the bank, and Jazz gets a little hysterical when he's left alone. Like I said, he's not well behaved. Not like yours." He bent down and patted Blackie's sides approvingly.

"Thank you," Mandy said, moving away in the direction of the howling dog. "Let's go and say hello to him, James."

"Thanks for buying Blackie a bone," James said, following Mandy.

They found the little terrier cowering under the long cloth of the merchant's table. The loop of his leather leash was tethered to the leg of the table. His head was thrown back, and his thin, nervous howling made Mandy's hair stand on end.

She bent down and lifted the cloth. "Hello, Jazz," she said softly. "Poor little thing! Your owner won't be away for long, you know."

The plump little dog backed away from her, lifted his chin, and let out another miserable wail.

"Ouch," James said, frowning. "My poor ears!" He tugged at Blackie's leash. He was trying to get under the table to look at the terrier, but James held him back. "Let's go, Mandy. We'll lose your parents if we're not careful."

"James," Mandy said, "it *is* the same sound, isn't it? It's just like the howling we heard in the night?"

"Sort of." James was hesitant.

"Well, you were asleep, that's obvious." Mandy chuckled. "It's exactly the same sound."

"So?" James asked.

"So," Mandy insisted, "it couldn't have been a fox

or an owl. That's my point. It was definitely a *dog*. Agreed?"

Before James could answer, Dr. Adam joined them. "Look at these!" he said. "I bought a pair of binoculars. Go on, let me treat you both to something!"

"Thanks, Dad," said Mandy. "I'd love an ice cream. How about you, James?"

"That would be fantastic," replied James.

"Fun, isn't it?" Dr. Emily said when she met them.

"What's going on over there?" Mandy craned her neck. A crowd had gathered in a circle to the left of them. She stood on tiptoe but couldn't see over the heads of the people jostling in front of her.

Drs. Adam and Emily edged closer, with Mandy and James just behind them. They came up against a metal barrier, behind which was a ring of sawdust. A glossy brown bull was cantering around in the ring, driven by the raised hand of a burly-looking farmer.

"Ah, an auction of farm animals," Dr. Adam said with interest.

"Dad." Mandy tugged at her father's jacket and he turned. "I don't really want to watch this. Can James and I go off and explore a bit on our own?"

"Certainly." Dr. Adam dug into his pants pocket and took out a few coins. "Take this for ice cream. Where should we meet?"

"There's the town's hall clock," Dr. Emily pointed out. "We'll meet you on the steps there at one o'clock."

"OK," Mandy agreed.

"Thanks, Dr. Adam." James grinned, jingling his coins. "See you later."

Mandy began to weave her way through the throng, away from the stalls.

"Where are we going?" James asked as he was tugged along by Blackie.

"I want to see if we can find out anything more about the dog on the heath," Mandy said.

"How?" James pushed his glasses up on his nose. "How are we going to do that?"

"I don't really know," she replied. "But we won't find out anything by standing around looking at cows in a ring, that's for sure. Let's explore the town first. We might find someone we can ask about it."

"OK," said James, warming to the idea. "We'll say that we're tourists — we've heard the story about the howling and want to know more. . . ."

"Look!" Mandy had stopped outside the window of a small bookshop. "There are all kinds of books in here about Dalton Heath."

James put his head to the window. "*A Tourists' Guide*," he read.

"*Mysteries of the Moor*," Mandy read the title of another dusty old volume excitedly. "Let's go in!"

"Do you think we should?" James said. "We don't have enough money to buy a book."

At that moment, the door of the shop opened and a white-haired old man looked out at them. "Come in," he muttered. "Come in and look around, if you want."

Mandy looked at James and raised her eyebrows. "Thank you," she said to the man, who nodded and shuffled back into the store.

James looped Blackie's leash around a metal boot scraper outside the door of the shop, where the dog sat down obediently to wait.

"Come on, James," Mandy urged. "He looks like the sort of man who would know everything there is to know about this place!"

With that, she pushed open the heavy wooden door and stepped inside.

Three

The musty-smelling old store was packed with ancient books. They teetered in piles on tables and lined the walls along wooden shelves that were buckled with age.

Mandy gaped as she looked around. "What a lot of old books," she whispered to James, who sneezed, then sniffed loudly. He shivered, and Mandy became aware that she, too, was suddenly very cold. Little of the warm autumn light was seeping in through the store window. It felt as though the place hadn't been heated in years.

"It's dusty in here. And where did the shopkeeper go?" James asked, sneezing loudly.

"He seems to have disappeared," Mandy murmured, surprised.

Cobwebs as thick as lace were festooned from the ceiling, draped like decorations. It was absolutely quiet, until Blackie whimpered outside. Mandy saw that he was pressing his nose to the grimy pane of glass in the lower half of the door to the shop.

"Let's go," James whispered. "Blackie's worried."

Mandy nodded. But, suddenly, something caught her eye. One of the big gray cobwebs on the ceiling seemed to tremble slightly. She kept on watching. It trembled again. Puzzled, she nudged James and pointed. Then the antique ceiling itself seemed to vibrate. Mandy blinked hard, not believing what she was seeing.

Suddenly, a flake of peeling paint detached itself and floated eerily to the floor.

"Let's go," James muttered again, more urgently this time.

But Mandy was rooted to the spot.

A door slammed and the sound of heavy footsteps echoed above their heads. The sloping shop ceiling shuddered and creaked.

"Someone's coming," she whispered. The sound of the slow and heavy tread ended with the groaning of a door. James and Mandy spun around to face the back of the gloomy store.

"And how may I help you?" whispered the shop-keeper.

He limped into the room and came up close, examining them as though they were specimens under a microscope. Looking at the jacket he was wearing and his gold pocket watch and chain, Mandy had the feeling that she'd somehow traveled back in time a hundred years or more.

"I'm Nicholas Moon — I own this shop," he said to them quietly, plucking at the wispy gray whiskers that hung from his chin.

"We saw a book in the window," Mandy began, her mouth dry, "about the moor — the *mysteries* of the moor."

"Ah, yes." Mr. Moon smiled suddenly and his cold blue eyes warmed. "A lot of tourists come in here wanting to know more about Dalton Heath. You are visitors, I suppose?"

James's glasses had slipped to the end of his nose and he pushed at them with a finger. "We're camping up on the heath," he said quickly.

"It's a peaceful place," Mr. Moon announced, picking his way carefully across the littered store and reaching in toward the window display. "Here it is. Is this the book you wanted?" He held it up. *"Mysteries of the Moor — A Study of Dalton Heath* by O. M. Penman."

Mandy nodded, her eyes shining. She couldn't wait to read the full story about the dog with the broken heart. Mr. Moon put the heavy book down on a dusty counter, and then retreated behind it. Instantly, James began to leaf through its pages. As he turned them, Mandy's face fell. The pages were filled with detailed pen-and-ink drawings of butterflies, birds, insects, and plants.

"Oh!" she said, disappointed.

"Oh?" said Mr. Moon, looking at her through the thick lenses of his round glasses. "Is it too expensive?"

"This is a nature book," James explained.

"Sort of," he agreed. "It tells you all about the unusual bird's-eye primrose and the globeflower, the rare white bogbean, and the extraordinary mystery of the tiny falcon called the merlin, which makes its home here on the moor."

"It's not really what we were looking for," Mandy said carefully, closing the book. "We were hoping to read about a different kind of mystery."

"By *mysteries*, you see, we meant . . . stories, legends, that sort of thing," James explained.

"I know what you mean," Mr. Moon said, suddenly looking rather angry. He folded his arms sternly across his jacket and stared at them piercingly. "Your heads are filled with silliness, like most of the people who come here. You want to know more about the story of the beast that's supposed to howl at night, don't you?" His voice had grown louder as he spoke and his blue eyes blazed.

"Beast?" said James in a small voice.

Mandy looked nervously at James. "We were only wondering about the story of the . . . dog . . ." she trailed off.

"It's all nonsense!" Mr. Moon declared angrily. "That's what I call it. I've lived here all my life and I've never heard so much as a whimper from the moor!"

James pushed the book back across the counter to Mr. Moon. "I'm sorry we bothered you," he mumbled.

"Now, look here, boy," Mr. Moon said, softening. He smiled gently, and Mandy thought he looked rather sad. "I don't mean to sound angry. It's just that this is the largest and finest stretch of heather moor in England. People should come here to appreciate that, rather than chasing after a wild story about strange animals crying in the night."

"So, it isn't true?" Mandy said wistfully.

"Of course it's *not true!*" Mr. Moon cried. "Why, I've never heard anything so ridiculous in my life."

"Well, thanks for your help," Mandy said quickly. "We won't take up any more of your time."

"Yes," James agreed. Mandy could see that he was

anxious to get out of the shop. Mr. Moon appeared very flustered. But suddenly he brightened.

"I know!" he said. "Let me show you a book about Boulby Cliff — the second highest sea cliff in England. Jurassic limestone cliffs — fascinating!" He drew a footstool toward him and climbed onto it with difficulty. "It's up here on this shelf. You'll be amazed when you see the pictures of . . ."

Mandy looked helplessly at James. "Let's beat it!" he whispered.

"James!" Mandy hissed. "We can't do that!"

"Here it is," said the old man, stepping back down with a book in his hand. "A wonderful book that tells about the coming of the Bronze Age settlers and . . ."

"Mr. Moon, we've really got to go now. Thanks for your trouble," Mandy said apologetically. She backed away toward the door and found that James had already pulled it open.

"Good-bye," Mandy called as she went out into the street.

"You won't find what you're looking for, you know," Mr. Moon yelled, shaking his head. "It's just a lot of silly nonsense!"

James stumbled into Mandy in his rush to get away. He grabbed Blackie's leash, and they hurried down the street. When they were out of sight of the store, James stopped to lean against a wall, wiping tears of laughter from his eyes.

"What a character," he said with a sigh.

"Poor old man," Mandy said sympathetically. "Don't laugh. Wouldn't you be fed up if everyone was more interested in a legend than your books?"

Blackie's tail was wagging hard. "It looks like there's an open field at the end of this street," Mandy pointed out. "Blackie deserves a good run. Should we take him?"

James looked at his watch. "We've got time," he said. He bent down to stroke Blackie. "You'd like that, wouldn't you, boy?"

Mandy began to run as James sprinted toward the field, Blackie straining ahead, his pink tongue lolling.

The town of Dalton gave way to a border of moorland that stretched as far as Mandy could see. When they'd left the streets of the old section behind them, James slipped off Blackie's leash and watched him bound away. The thirsty dog plunged down the grassy bank of a small stream, stopping to lap its clear water. Beyond the stream, the land rose steadily and steeply, culminating in a craggy cliff at its crest.

"I bet we could walk back to our camp from here," James said.

"You think so?" Mandy grinned. "Which direction?"

"Well, I'm not sure," James admitted, squinting up at the sky to check the position of the sun. "But our Land Rover is just north of the town, and we are walking due north of the town right now, so it can't be hard to find."

"Thank goodness I'm with a Boy Scout!" teased Mandy. "Anyway," she added, "Dad's got the Land Rover, so we won't need to walk. Besides, we've got to meet in the town square."

Blackie was quivering with excitement. He'd picked up the scent of moorland animals and was darting here and there, his nose to the ground.

"Let's follow this bridle path," Mandy suggested, enjoying the feel of the springy turf under her feet. "It's marked with an old stone cross."

James paused to look at the cross, which was almost as tall as he was. MACARTHUR'S POINT was written on it in black paint.

"I wonder who MacArthur was?" James mused. "This cross probably marks his grave. I'll bet a Viking ran him to ground and . . ."

"Oh, shush," said Mandy. "Let's not talk about how the poor man died. If he did die, that is."

James walked together with Mandy. Blackie raced ahead and, from time to time, he paused to make certain he hadn't lost sight of his owner.

The path led them away from the town, rising high in places, then dropping away on the left into the dales.

"This is great." Mandy took a deep breath of crisp air. "It's so empty . . . and wild!"

"I wouldn't like to get lost here, though." James shivered. "There's nobody around."

"You know, Mr. Moon was right," Mandy said suddenly. "We should appreciate the moor for what it is. It's beautiful — and it's nice to think that it's a place where so many animals can live safely."

"Well, I think we have a better chance of coming across an otter than a strange howling animal." James chuckled.

"You can say what you like," Mandy said quietly, "but I *did* hear howling last night. And I'm sure it was a dog. It *certainly* didn't sound anything like a fox or an owl."

"All right, all right!" James laughed. "But you heard what Mr. Moon said. The story about the dog is just a lot of nonsense to attract the tourists."

"Yes, well, maybe." Mandy still wasn't convinced. "But I *know* that I heard what I heard," she added.

"Where's Blackie?" James stopped suddenly and put a hand to his face to shield his eyes from the strange, pale light from the sky. "He was there a minute ago."

Mandy and James looked fearfully at each other, and Mandy felt a shiver run through her body. "Oh, James," she wailed. "Don't say we've lost him! There are lots of bogs around here."

"Don't worry," James said quickly. "He's probably down in the dip of that dale. Come on — I'm sure he'll be fine." He ran off at once, with a worried look on his face. Mandy hurried after him.

In the depths of the dale below them, there stood a clump of conifers, a thicket of no more than fifty trunks. Beyond the trees, the land began to rise again steeply.

"I bet he's gone after a rabbit." Mandy puffed, thrusting her hands into the pockets of her sweater. "Oh, James, we can't lose him! Not out here!"

"Blackie!" James shouted. "Here, boy."

"Quickly," Mandy urged. "Let's not go into the thicket, though. It might be dangerous."

James started running, shouting for his dog.

Then, after a few seconds, Blackie appeared out of the thicket, looking very sheepish. His tail swished rather hesitantly from side to side. He was panting after his dash around the dale, but stood still, his head to one side, looking up at them expectantly.

James and Mandy both heaved a huge sigh of relief. "Here!" James repeated sternly, swinging the leash.

"Oh, James!" Mandy said in dismay as the Labrador came closer. "He's filthy!"

Blackie's four legs were coated in thick, black mud.

He wagged his tail proudly. "Oh, no! Where could he have been to get that muddy?" James wondered, wrinkling his nose.

"I don't know." Mandy frowned, looking around her.

"Let's head back," James suggested. "We'll wash Blackie in the little stream that we saw earlier."

"Good idea," Mandy answered. "I don't want to share our tent with him tonight in that state!"

They started back the way they had come, climbing steadily along the path. James walked ahead, with Blackie to heel. When the sun broke unexpectedly through the cloud, Mandy paused to look back down toward the pretty, little thicket, set like an island in the middle of a sea of lilac-colored heather.

She was so surprised by what she saw that, for a moment, she couldn't find her voice to alert James. There was a bench to the left of the trees, and on it was a man, sitting tall and straight and still. He seemed to be looking right at Mandy. Yet neither of them had noticed him sitting there before.

Not taking her curious gaze from his, she reached out and tugged James's sleeve. "Look," she said in a low voice.

James pushed his hair away from his forehead and followed her gaze.

"Where did he pop up from? I didn't notice him ear-

lier," he whispered, whipping off his glasses and polishing them on his T-shirt. "Wait a minute . . . is it a man, or a statue?"

"It's a man," Mandy whispered, feeling strangely shaken by the man's appearance. "Isn't it odd? I didn't see him, either. We must have passed right by him on our way toward the trees."

"Well, he's probably a bird-watcher or something," James reasoned. "Perhaps he's been sneaking around, trying not to scare the merlins, or whatever Mr. Moon said there were up here. Perhaps he brought his own bench."

"Don't be silly!" Mandy hissed.

She crouched down, pretending to be fiddling with the lace on her sneaker, but keeping an eye on the man, who looked back solemnly at her. He sat very still, his knees together, his hands in his lap, staring at them in a way Mandy found very disturbing. On his face was an expression of deep sadness.

"I wonder if there's something wrong with him," she murmured. "He looks very pale."

"What?" James bent down beside her. "Mandy, I feel like an idiot — what *are* you doing?"

"Watching," Mandy explained. "Perhaps he's ill."

"Crazy, more like it," James whispered. "I don't like

the way he's staring at us. We'd better get up and go on, or he'll think *we're* nuts." James stood up and put his hand on Blackie's collar. He gave a little tug. "Come on, boy." But Blackie remained where he was. His ears were pricked, his hackles high. He stared at the man intently, though he was not growling.

"Blackie! Mandy!" James pleaded. "This has nothing to do with *us*. Let's —"

"James!" Mandy interrupted. "He's calling us over! Look, he wants us to go to him!"

Mandy stood up, shielding her eyes as the low cloud suddenly parted to reveal a brilliant sun. She looked hard at the figure on the bench. As she watched, he raised a hand and beckoned again.

"Hello?" Mandy called out boldly. "Can we help you?"

"Oh, *Mandy!*" James said, exasperated. "*Now* you've done it."

There was silence from the bench. For a third time, he lifted a pale hand and slowly and deliberately curled his fingers, calling them nearer. Blackie looked up at James and whined.

"This is a bit creepy," James declared. "Blackie doesn't like it — he's acting very strangely. Look at him."

"Well, I'm going to find out what he wants," Mandy said. "He might be in trouble or something."

"He looks perfectly all right, Mandy," James said. "I don't think . . ."

But Mandy didn't hear the rest of his sentence. She had boldly started off back down the path, her curiosity drawing her closer to the strange, silent figure on the bench.

Four

As Mandy approached the bench, she glanced back over her shoulder. To her relief, she saw that James and Blackie were following. James was scowling fiercely and looking at his watch.

At that moment, the morning sun suddenly disappeared behind a dark, overhanging cloud, casting a dull gray haze over the heath. Moments before, the moor had seemed a welcoming place, but now Mandy was filled with a sense of foreboding. She shivered as a brisk little wind began to blow around her. It moaned through the trees in the thicket and tugged at her hair.

"Hello," she called out as she approached, her voice

quavering nervously. The man's arms lay limply at his sides. She noticed that his skin had a peculiar transparency about it. He wore baggy, khaki-colored trousers held up by a pair of wide suspenders, and there was a bulky cloth bag tied with a drawstring resting against his boots. He was young, no more than eighteen or so, she guessed, though from a distance he had appeared older, sitting so still on the seat. His face was troubled as he lifted his pale, searching eyes to hers.

"Come a little closer," he said in a low, rasping tone. Mandy hesitated and looked back for James. Blackie had decided to sit down, and she saw that James was

pulling on the leather leash, looking alternately frustrated and alarmed.

Mandy stepped closer. "Are you . . . lost?" she asked carefully. The man leaned forward, and, at first, didn't speak. Mandy recoiled at his silence. Butterflies had started fluttering nervously in her stomach. She knew it was unwise to talk to strangers, but her good sense was often overruled by her need to help where she could. And, she'd come this far, she reasoned with herself. There was no backing out now. If she turned and fled, he would think she was rude.

"Not me." The young man spoke so softly, it was as though his voice was coming from a great distance. "I'm looking for my dog."

"Oh!" she said, automatically following his gaze as he looked out across the moor. She thought that the blended colors of lilac, green, and brown gave it the look of a huge watercolor painting, but there was nothing resembling an animal to be seen anywhere. "Has he been gone long?"

The man's strange, pale eyes were fixed intently on her face. "Oh, yes," he murmured, and shook his head.

Mandy made herself relax. He was an animal lover like herself. He'd probably walked a great distance across the moors, calling for his beloved pet. He was tired and hoarse from shouting.

"I've been all over, you see. And I'm so tired," the young man continued wearily. "But I can't rest until I find him." He rubbed the bristly, close-cropped hair on his head and looked up hopefully at Mandy.

"Of course not!" Mandy agreed. She knew that she wouldn't be able to rest for a minute should Blackie have become lost on the moor. She was sorry to have to disappoint him. "My friend and I have walked quite far from the town," she told him. "We haven't seen anyone, not even a dog, until we spotted you." She turned as James came up. "This is James. I'm Mandy." Blackie was lying a short distance away, with his leash coiled on the ground beside him and his ears pricked.

"That dog will *not* listen to me," James grumbled. "He's behaving very stubbornly. Hello." He nodded to the man on the bench.

"He's looking for his dog," Mandy explained. "It's lost on the moors, poor thing."

"Oh, wow," said James, looking doubtful. "That's not good. It's so huge."

"Rover," the young man said in his strange, whispery voice. "The dog's name is Rover. He must be around here somewhere. . . ." He broke off, frowning.

"Oh, I'm sure he is," Mandy said soothingly. "He'll come back, you'll see."

"Is that your dog?" he asked James suddenly, pointing at Blackie.

"Yes, that's my Blackie." James sounded proud. "He's usually quite sociable, only today he refuses to come any closer. I don't know what's wrong with him."

The young man smiled slightly. "Who knows?" he said.

"Was your Rover on a leash?" Mandy asked.

"No," he said sadly. "I left him at home when I went out, you see —"

"And he's wandered off!" Mandy butted in sympathetically. "Why do you think he'll be here, then — on the moor, I mean?"

"He's here." He nodded. "I'm sure of it."

"Well, what does Rover look like?" Mandy continued brightly, determined to be helpful.

"Pale gray, but he can look almost honey-colored in some lights. I think," he added, looking dreamily at the horizon.

James caught Mandy's eye and quickly circled his forefinger level with his eyebrows, signaling to her that he thought this guy was obviously crazy.

"We'll keep a lookout for him," James said, turning away. "We've got to go, now, because Mandy's parents . . ."

"Lovely long muzzle, a gentle dog, a good friend . . ." the man went on, as if James hadn't spoken.

James put his hands on his hips, glaring in annoyance at Mandy. "Don't we, Mandy?" he repeated. "Have to go now, I mean?"

"He was as faithful as could be." The man seemed lost in the memories of Rover. His voice was becoming even more strained. "Never left my side, not if he could help it."

Mandy couldn't help staring curiously at the young man. There was something peculiar about him, that was certain. She jumped nervously at a rustling behind her, and turned to see Blackie slowly sidling up toward them. His brown eyes were fixed on the figure on the bench, unblinking. He approached cautiously, half-crouching, as though he was stalking an uncertain prey.

"Hello, there," whispered the stranger when he noticed the Labrador. "Hello, boy. Come on, then — come and say hello."

Blackie's hackles were up, and his nose worked overtime as he tried to identify a scent that he could recognize. He came within inches of the young man's long, pale, outstretched fingers — and then tucked his tail between his legs, jerked away, and bolted back up the hill.

"Blackie!" James shouted, going after him. "Don't be so *silly*! What on Earth is the matter with you today?"

"We'd better go now," Mandy said reluctantly. "I hope you find your dog. We'll keep a lookout for him."

The man sat staring after Blackie and didn't reply. He turned his mournful eyes back to her and sighed.

"Um . . . good-bye, then," Mandy said.

"Good-bye," he said. "I'll be here, waiting."

"Waiting?" Mandy frowned.

"In case Rover comes," he replied. "I'll just sit here and wait. Good-bye."

Mandy nodded, smiling, then turned and ran to join James.

"Phew!" she said, expelling her breath in a rush of confusion and nervousness. "What an *odd* man!"

"Well, I don't know why you had to go and talk to him," James scolded, hurrying after Blackie. "He's obviously lost his marbles. He was just babbling. . . . I don't think there *is* a dog!"

"James!" Mandy was disappointed. "How would *you* feel if Blackie wandered off across this enormous moor and got lost? Wouldn't you want someone to help you find him?"

"I don't think he *has* a dog," James said again, stooping to snatch at Blackie's trailing leash. "He had difficulty remembering what it looked like. I think he was making it all up!"

"Maybe he just wasn't very good at describing things," Mandy murmured, defending the sad young man.

"Well, I think he's a crackpot." James scowled. "I'm hungry, Mandy, and we're late. We said we'd meet your parents."

"OK, I'm coming," Mandy said.

They had reached the rise of the hill where she had first spotted the man on the bench. She couldn't resist a furtive glance behind her. She paused and turned. The gathering cloud was the color of an old bruise, blotting out the sun and making the moor seem less friendly.

In the gloom, Mandy could barely see the little bench in the dale below. And there was no sign of the man who had sat there a minute earlier. "He's gone!" she exclaimed.

"Who?" James turned.

"The *man*!" Mandy said as patiently as she could. "Look, the bench is empty. He said he would wait."

"Well, he's wandered off home, or somewhere. Come on, Mandy. Let's forget about him and his imaginary dog, and just get back to the town. I've had enough of strange people today."

"OK," Mandy agreed. There was surely a reasonable

explanation for the man's odd behavior. But she was not likely to see him again. She and James had only two more days to enjoy the moors — she would put it all out of her head and focus on having a good time.

"You're right," she said, linking her arm through his. "Let's just forget about it. Look, there's the stream. We'd better hurry — Mom and Dad will be starting to worry!"

Five

"Where *have* you been?" Mandy saw her father's worried frown lift with relief when he saw her. "You're nearly half an hour late."

Mandy was out of breath from her dash back into town from the heath. "Sorry, Dad!" she gasped, bending over double.

"Really sorry, Dr. Adam," James puffed, sweeping his hair out of his eyes. "We lost track of the time. We were . . . exploring!"

Dr. Emily laughed. "Exploring? There are only two streets in the entire town, James."

"Stores and things . . ." Mandy explained vaguely. It

was just as well not to mention that she and James had been out across part of the heath alone, and had a conversation with a rather peculiar stranger.

"And the heath," James said, "it's just over there." He pointed. "At the end of that street. We thought Blackie might like a run."

"Well," Dr. Adam grumbled, "you're here now and Mom and I are starving! How would you like to have lunch?"

"Yes, please!" James said approvingly. "Blackie must be thirsty, too."

"OK." Dr. Emily smiled and smoothed Blackie's head. "He looks a bit downhearted, James. There's nothing wrong with him, is there?"

Mandy looked at James, wishing that Blackie would perk up and wag his tail or something. He'd been behaving strangely ever since the encounter with the young man out on the heath. Mandy hoped it wouldn't attract too many questions from her sharp-eyed mother. The Labrador's head was low, his pink tongue showing as he panted steadily. For once, he was showing none of his usual boisterous curiosity and delight at being out with James and Mandy.

James tugged at the leash and Blackie looked up. "Lunch!" James told him enthusiastically. "And a nice drink of cold water. Come on, boy!" Blackie obligingly wagged his tail. "Look, Dr. Emily, he's fine, see? Just a bit tired I guess."

Dr. Adam began striding down the street in the direction of the restaurant, which bore a brass sign announcing its name — THE GRUBBY DUCK. Inside, they found a table near a window.

"Ah, that's nice," Dr. Emily said, sinking into a chair. "We seem to have walked miles!"

"Look, James! There's a stream running through the garden!" Mandy was pressing her nose to the pane, peering out on a carefully tended lawn bordered by an expanse of clear water. James finished attaching Blackie's leash to the table leg and looked out.

"Oh, great! Let's have a stick race a little later," he suggested, his eyes shining. "That water is flowing pretty fast."

"I'd leave Blackie in here," Dr. Emily added, lifting the cloth to look under the table. "He's having a well-earned snooze."

After lunch, Mandy and James went out the side door and down a few stone steps onto a paved terrace. There were tables and chairs under a striped awning, but it was no longer warm enough for customers to sit outdoors. A big tabby cat was curled around a shriveled stem in a plant pot, sleeping. Mandy tried to pet it, but it leaped up in alarm, hissing, and shot off around the corner.

"Probably wild," James announced as Mandy looked after it, disappointed.

"What a gorgeous little river!" she said. The water was crystal clear and only a yard or so deep. It splashed and gurgled on its way downstream, tugging with some force at the plants that grew along its banks.

"Ducks! Over there." James pointed. "They don't look particularly grubby to me," he said, chuckling at his own joke.

"Let's hunt for sticks," Mandy said, wandering away upstream. She followed the bank, heading for a leafless tree that was silhouetted starkly against the white wall of the restaurant. Paddling furiously against the flow of the water, the ducks followed, quacking loudly.

"What a noise!" Mandy giggled, admiring the glossy green of the mallards' heads. "It's no use — I haven't got *any* bread for you!"

Then she stopped and frowned. The ducks had fallen silent when she'd spoken, and she had distinctly heard a mewing sound. Mandy looked around her, baffled. It was a tiny sound, faint but insistent, and it made her heart race.

There was no mistaking it — the frantic, continuous sound of mewing. It seemed to be coming from the opposite bank. She looked across the water, her eye drawn by the bobbing of a discarded bag of chips, and gasped.

A tiny gray kitten was clinging to a little heap of twigs and bracken! Even as Mandy looked in horror, the kitten's raft was being broken up by the current. In one heart-stopping moment, she saw its panic-stricken eyes and the pink of its tongue as it mewed again in terror. One fragile back leg was already trailing in the water!

"Did you find some? Twigs, I mean?" James called.

But Mandy didn't reply. She sprang from the bank and landed on the stony bottom of the riverbed with a noisy splash. Then she desperately began wading across to the opposite bank as quickly as she could, using her hands as paddles to propel her toward the kitten. The water was freezing cold — she drew in her breath sharply as it lapped around her waist.

"Mandy!" She heard James shout in astonishment.

"Get Mom and Dad, James — hurry!" Mandy shouted, plunging on through the water, knowing that by yelling to him, she was frightening the kitten even more. The tiny animal shrank from the approaching stranger. Then it let go of the slender branch that it clung to and tried to edge backward to escape.

"Don't, please . . . it's all right. I won't hurt you," she said softly.

Just as Mandy reached the small raft of sticks, weeds, and bracken, the kitten tried to jump to safety, missed its footing and tumbled into the stream.

"Oh, no!" Mandy wailed. As she groped around des- perately under the water, she saw the kitten bob up — just a bedraggled little face and two wide eyes, blinking helplessly. Mandy made a grab for it, desperate to save the kitten before the current carried it away down- stream. It came up in her hands, as light as a feather, sneezing. Mandy could feel its frail little bones through the sodden fur.

"What is it? Hold on! I'm coming, Mandy!" Dr. Adam bellowed from the bank, and Mandy turned to see the alarmed look on her father's face as he scrabbled to open the clasp of his watch.

"No, it's all right, Dad!" she shouted. "I'm coming out. I've got it."

"Got what?" Dr. Emily was tugging urgently at her shoelaces.

Mandy had tucked the kitten inside her sweater, up against her pounding heart. She had begun to shiver with cold. "It's a kitten," she chattered as her father put out a hand to haul her out of the river. "It almost drowned."

"Oh, Mandy!" Dr. Emily shook her head at the sight of her dripping daughter. "You'll catch a horrible cold! Quick, come inside, and bring the kitten with you."

"Is it going to be all right, Dad? Mom?" She peeled back her sweater as Dr. Adam bent to take a closer look.

"Poor little thing," he murmured, opening the kitten's mouth. "Yes, I think it'll be fine. But it's a good thing you got the kitten out when you did, sweetie."

James put out a finger to pet the kitten. "I can see its pink skin right through the fur," he observed.

Mandy pulled her sweater over the kitten's head and began to run back to the restaurant. "Come on, James," she said. "We'll take it inside."

A crowd of people had gathered on the terrace. As she hurried toward them, they craned their necks to see what Mandy had in her arms. Among them was a girl who Mandy guessed was about her age. Her brown hair was a tangle of curls, and she had freckles across the bridge of her nose.

"What is it?" she asked Mandy, wrinkling her nose. "It isn't one of those big toads, is it?"

"No, it's a kitten," she replied. "It fell into the stream."

"Oh!" The girl covered her mouth with her hand. "Bring it in — my mom and dad own the restaurant. They won't mind."

"Thanks," James said.

Mandy handed the kitten to her mother. "I can't go in, I'm dripping wet."

"You can borrow some of my things, if you like," the girl said, shyly. "We're about the same size."

"That's very nice of you." Dr. Emily smiled. "She does look frozen in those wet things."

Mandy's lips had turned a muddy mauve color, and she trembled all over. The girl dashed away. "Hurry up inside," she called. "It's only water, so nothing will get ruined."

Mandy took off her sneakers and socks and squeezed the water out of her jeans as best she could. Inside, she found that her mother had the kitten in her lap. It spat and coughed and shook its head, all the while trying to escape Dr. Emily's grasp. Beside her, Blackie was staring down at the struggling animal with great interest. Mandy kept off the carpet. Her jeans dripped steadily onto the wide flagstone hearth.

"Oh, it's cute!" James said, gently touching the shivering kitten.

Dr. Emily smiled. "It seems like a lively little cat. I'm sure it'll survive."

"How old is it, Mom?" Mandy asked.

"Um . . . about four weeks, I'd guess," she replied, looking at the kitten's teeth.

"Here you go," said the girl, springing to Mandy's side with a bundle of clothing. "You can go into the coatroom and change, over there." She pointed. "I'm Hayley, by the way."

"I'm Mandy, and this is my friend James. Thanks so much."

Minutes later, Mandy had changed into warm, dry clothes. Hayley had provided a pair of leggings, a long-sleeved T-shirt, a sweater, and a pair of wool socks, as well as a big plastic bag for Mandy's wet things. In the restaurant, Dr. Adam was carefully examining the mewing kitten for signs of injury. The restaurant was getting busier, and the group huddled around the kitten was attracting curious stares.

"It's had a lucky escape." Dr. Adam smiled.

"Lucky!" said Hayley, stroking the kitten's head. "That's what I'll call him!"

"Is this *your* kitten?" James asked, shifting his glasses higher up his nose.

"Not really," Hayley admitted. "But he might as well be. You see, I've been feeding a stray cat and I *thought* that she looked as though she was going to have kittens."

"So . . ." Mandy looked up, frowning. "If this is one of her litter, then there might be others!"

"Oh," Hayley said, "I didn't think of that."

"Where is she? The mother cat?" James asked.

"She comes and goes. I don't really know," Hayley admitted. "I haven't seen her around for a while." She put out a finger to Lucky, who, after his frightening adventure, had closed his eyes and was snuggled safely in the warmth of Dr. Emily's lap.

"We'd better go and take a look," Mandy said. "If Lucky was near the river, the others might be in danger of falling in, too, don't you think?"

"I suppose so," Hayley agreed, looking worried.

"Can I go, Mom? Dad?" Mandy looked from one to the other.

Dr. Adam nodded. "OK. Go!" He grinned. "Mom and I will keep an eye on Lucky here. But I can't promise not to eat your share of the ice cream!"

"And be careful!" added Dr. Emily as Mandy, James, and Hayley dashed out the door. Mandy's shoes squeaked as she walked, the dampness soaking quickly into her borrowed socks.

"My guess is," James said while he wagged his finger, "that the rest of the litter will be on the opposite bank, where Mandy found Lucky."

"I don't like the idea of another swim!" Mandy shuddered.

"You don't have to swim — there's a bridge a little farther down," Hayley said brightly. "I'll show you."

It was a wooden bridge, held together by iron struts. They crossed and spread out, treading carefully through the undergrowth. Mandy searched the riverbank, her eyes peeled for the slightest movement and her ears straining for the tiniest sound of mewing.

Suddenly, James shouted. "Over here!"

He was on his knees, looking in a rusty, old metal drum. It lay on its side, propped up by the jutting roots of a tree, partially covered by a curtain of vines. It was dangerously close to where the river water was lapping at the bank.

"Oh!" gasped Hayley, crouching down beside him. "Just look!"

Four gray kittens were curled up inside the drum. They were fast asleep, knitted together in a tangle of legs and paws and tiny pink noses, so that Mandy couldn't tell where one ended and another began.

"I'm *so* glad we've found them," she whispered. "Look how close the drum is to the water!"

"Just a few adventurous steps and they might have fallen in!" James said, horrified.

"The mother cat's not here," Mandy noticed, looking around.

"I'm going to ask my mom and dad if I can look after them!" Hayley stood up, her eyes shining. "They can't stay here — it's not safe!"

"Oh, good idea!" Mandy grinned. "We could come back with a cardboard box and get them . . . and maybe even tempt the mother cat to join them."

"Yes!" Hayley was glowing. "Come on," she urged, starting back for the bridge. "There's no time to lose."

Mandy's parents were having coffee and chatting with Mrs. Roberts, the restaurant owner. She had the same springy curls as her daughter, which fell in waves around her face as she bent to look at Lucky. The little kitten was still fast asleep.

"Mom!" Hayley yelled, rushing up to the table. "We've found the rest of the litter! There are four of them — they're sleeping in an oil drum right beside the riverbank. Oh, Mom, could we . . . can I . . . ?"

"I *thought* this would happen!" Mrs. Roberts said knowingly, winking at Mandy. "From the moment she started to feed the stray —"

"Can I, Mom? Please!" Hayley begged, cutting her mother short.

"Yes, all right!" Mrs. Roberts laughed. "But don't expect *me* to take care of them. I've got enough to do as it is. You're responsible, OK? And you'll have to find suitable homes for them, when they're older."

"I promise," Hayley said happily. "Are there any cardboard boxes in the kitchen? I can make a bed for the kittens." With that, she hurried off.

"They're the prettiest little things," Mandy said longingly, sitting beside her father. James took a sip of his orange juice.

"This restaurant seems to attract needy animals," Mrs. Roberts said. "Last year, we found that a young badger had taken up residence in our outside storeroom!"

"It's a lovely, wild part of the world," Dr. Adam said. "We're camping on the heath. Great scenery."

Mrs. Roberts cleared her throat. "You haven't been kept awake at night, have you?" she asked mysteriously.

Mandy sat bolt upright and knocked over James's glass, which was now empty. She grabbed it and set it back on the table.

"We've heard about the legend." Dr. Adam grimaced. "And we're *trying* not to pay attention to it." He glared playfully at Mandy.

Mandy looked up eagerly at Mrs. Roberts as she came and stood beside their table. "Why do you ask?" she said.

Mrs. Roberts narrowed her eyes and glanced quickly from side to side. "Many of the campers have come in here and told me they've been awakened by the sound of eerie howling."

"Really?" said Dr. Emily, looking surprised. "We thought it was just a legend."

"No, I don't think so." Mrs. Roberts shook her head gravely and lowered her voice. "Too many people have heard it — there must be some truth to it."

"So you haven't heard it yourself?" asked Dr. Adam with a twinkle in his eyes.

"No, but . . ." Mrs. Roberts looked uneasy. "One night

a few years ago, the local animal refuge searched the moor," Mrs. Roberts remembered. "They found nothing. Not a trace. And the howling has been heard for so many years now — what sort of animal could have lived so long? Certainly not a dog."

Mandy looked at James. It seemed that his suspicions had been correct.

Everyone was silent, waiting for Mrs. Roberts to go on.

"They say that it howls only at night, and always from a particular spot on the heath, somewhere up near MacArthur's Point. Some claim that it's the ghost of an animal caught in a trap, others that it drowned in a bog on the moor. Of course," she said, "some people swear they've seen the animal quite clearly — it's got pointed ears and fangs, dripping blood."

"Oh, no!" Dr. Emily chuckled. "That's going a bit far!"

"Yes," Mrs. Roberts agreed.

"We read in a guidebook that some people believe it's just a dog that died pining for its lost master," Mandy said.

Mrs. Roberts nodded. "That's what our Olive says, and I'm inclined to believe her."

"Olive?" Mandy felt her excitement mounting. "Who's Olive?"

"Olive's my great-*great*-grandmother — my nana,"

Hayley piped up, coming back to the table. "She knows all about Dalton Heath — more than anyone!"

Mrs. Roberts laughed. "Nana will keep you busy for hours I expect — if you find her awake, that is!"

"Can we talk to her, Hayley?" Mandy's eyes were shining. "Nana — Olive, I mean?"

"Sure." Hayley looked pleased. "I'll take you upstairs to meet her. But do you mind if we make sure the kittens are safe first?"

"Let's hurry," Mandy said. "They might have decided to start exploring!"

Six

The kittens were up by the time Mandy, James, and Hayley returned to their den. They were tumbling and playing, but staying well within the limits of the steel drum.

"Thank goodness they're not brave enough to venture out yet," Mandy said as she crouched down and looked inside. The treacherous water of the rushing stream lay less than a yard away.

James put down the cardboard box he was carrying. Mrs. Roberts had lined it with newspaper and an old woolen blanket. "I wish the mother cat was here," he

64

said, looking around. "I feel as if we're robbing her of her babies!"

"Me, too," Hayley agreed. "But I'm sure she'll come looking for them at the restaurant."

"We could lure her to them with a trail of dry cat food," Mandy suggested. She crept closer to the kittens. Startled by the noise of her approach, they arched their backs and tried to look as threatening as they could.

"It's OK," Mandy murmured, reaching in to lift the gray kitten closest to her. It gazed up at her with wide eyes, then gave a fierce little rumbling growl and spat. Mandy tried to soothe it against her chest, but it struggled, its claws outstretched. The other three were huddled together, their expressions fearful.

Hayley lifted the palest of the litter, while James put the remaining two in the cardboard box. They sniffed at the blanket and tried to hide under its folds.

"It's horrible to think how much we're scaring them." Mandy sighed. "I wish they could understand that we're trying to help."

"They can't," James said gently. "But I'm sure they'll love their new life. It'll be so much nicer than living in this rusty old tin can on the edge of a river." He patted Mandy's arm, adding, "Don't worry."

"OK," said Hayley, standing with the box in her arms.

The sound of pitiful mewing rose up from its depths. "Poor little things! Let's go."

But James stood still, his mouth agape, pointing.

It was the mother cat. She had been alerted by the frantic calling of her litter. Her tail twitched and her eyes burned at them from where she stood, half hidden by a tree. She was terribly thin, Mandy saw, and it was plain that she couldn't decide whether to flee from the strangers or attack. She crouched low, giving off a menacing growl.

"Let's go," Mandy said. "I bet she'll follow her babies."

They set off at a quick pace. The mewing increased in intensity as the kittens in the jolting box wailed for their mother. She followed at a distance, slinking from tree to tree, as though she were trying to take cover from an enemy. She darted over the bridge and kept up a loping gait all the way back to the restaurant.

"Hooray!" said Hayley when James reported that she was still following. "Our plan has worked."

In The Grubby Duck, Drs. Adam and Emily were finishing their coffee. A gentle purr could be heard nearby. Lucky's fur had dried to a soft gray, and he was now awake, lying in the nest of Mandy's mother's cardigan on a big armchair and licking carefully at his paws.

"He's fine." Dr. Emily smiled. "Doing really well.

Look, he's sprucing himself up. Have you got the rest of the litter?"

Triumphantly, Hayley lowered the box. "Aren't they gorgeous?" she said.

"Nothing wrong with their vocal chords," Dr. Adam observed, putting his fingers in his ears.

"The mother cat followed us," Mandy said. "She's hanging around outside. She's quite upset."

"Understandably," Dr. Emily said. "It might be best to take the box out to her. Put it someplace sheltered — and put out a little food for her, too."

Very carefully, Mandy plucked Lucky from his perch on the chair. He yowled with fright, grabbing her sweater with his claws. Mandy lowered him gently into the box with his brothers and sisters.

On the terrace outside, there was a low stone bench. Hayley placed the box underneath it, in a pool of watery sunshine, up against the wall of the restaurant. There was just enough space between the lip of the box and the base of the bench for the mother cat to get in beside her litter. Then, after Hayley, Mandy, and James put out a saucer of milk and some dry cat food, they stood back to admire a job well done.

"She'll be pleased," James said, "when she finds them in there, all safe and sound."

"Thanks for your help," Hayley said.

The mother cat was lying under a bush. Her anxious eyes never left the cardboard box.

"If we go away, she might get in with them," Mandy reasoned. "Let's go and visit your great-great-grandmother, OK?"

They climbed the staircase to the first floor of the Roberts's house. The buzz of chattering and the clink of dishes in the busy restaurant grew fainter with each step. A patterned carpet in red and gold led off to several closed doors that Mandy guessed were the bedrooms.

"Nana doesn't go out much anymore," Hayley explained as she knocked and opened one of the doors. "Her legs aren't so good these days. She likes to keep warm and look out at the moor — and remember."

"Will she mind our coming like this?" James asked cautiously.

"Oh, no, Nana loves seeing people," Hayley replied. "You should have brought your dog."

"Blackie's gone with Mandy's parents," James said. "He wouldn't miss the chance for a walk around the town."

"He's a lovely dog," Hayley remarked. Then she called out, "Nana!"

Mandy and James followed her to a large, cozily furnished living room. At first, Mandy couldn't see anybody in the room, but then she became aware of a very small, white-haired old lady. She was sitting in a leather armchair, looking out of the window in front of her at the expanse of moor. She half turned and smiled at Hayley.

"Hello, my dear," she said warmly.

"Nana, these are my new friends, Mandy and James. They're camping on the heath," Hayley began, slipping to her knees at the foot of the chair. "Mandy and James, this is my grandmother, Olive Johnston Roberts."

Olive Roberts smiled gently and held up a hand that was gnarled with age, like the trunk of an ancient tree.

Mandy came forward shyly and took the old lady's fingers. There was a scent of lavender and violets rising from the shawl around her frail shoulders. Her eyes, she noticed, were the strong blue of sapphires, twinkling merrily in a face that was creased with age.

"Sit down," she invited in a whispery voice. "Are you having a good vacation?"

"Yes, thank you," James answered, kneeling beside Hayley on the carpet. Mandy did the same, so that the three of them formed a semicircle at Olive's feet.

Mandy couldn't remain silent for another moment. "We heard that there is a legend about these moors," she said eagerly. "Could you tell us the story about

the animal that howls at night?" She hoped that Olive wouldn't dismiss the tale as tourist bait, the way Mr. Moon had.

The old lady sighed dreamily and allowed her gaze to travel out of the window once more. For a second, Mandy wondered if she had forgotten her question, but then she began to speak.

"No one else knows the real story," she began. "I'm the only one who can remember what really happened now."

"Of course, Nana," Hayley said protectively.

"My brother could have told you, if he'd been here." She looked at the floor, slowly shaking her head. Olive took a deep breath and folded her hands in her lap.

James shifted uncomfortably on the carpet. He caught Mandy's eye. She frowned at him, willing him to be patient as the old lady went on.

"It's the saddest sound in the world, that howling," she whispered. "The poor creature went on and on, haunting the night with its terrible wailing, like a thing possessed . . ." Olive trailed off, then coughed delicately into a small lace handkerchief and blinked back a sudden rush of tears.

Mandy caught James's eye. He was hugging his knees. She could tell that he was anxious to hear more about the haunted heath.

"It was the sound of mourning, or a cry of pain . . . the

pain of longing," she spoke mysteriously, her dim old eyes glazing over. She gazed out across the moor, a faraway look in her eyes, as though there was no one in the room with her. One silvery tear slipped down her cheek.

Hayley reached up and squeezed her nana's frail hand. "You look tired — should we go?"

"Oh! But the story . . ." Mandy pleaded.

"They make up stories, for the visitors, you know. But I know the real story." Olive seemed not to have heard Hayley's question. "The dog lived on the moor, hunting by day and howling for its master at night. It died of a broken heart when it was abandoned by the person it loved the most in the world."

So it really *was* a dog! Mandy looked quickly at James, then slowly shook her head. "How sad," she whispered, adding, "and people *still* hear it?"

The wisps of Olive's snowy hair lay on her forehead like cobwebs. The old lady looked weary and confused. Her eyes closed momentarily, then fluttered open. "They say so." She nodded. "It's a long time since I've been up on the heath. I've heard it's just skin and bones now, but still proud and unapproachable. They've tried to find it and bring it in, but it's clever." Olive chuckled, half to herself. Her eyes burned brightly. "They'll never catch it. It's waiting, you see."

"Waiting?" James whispered.

"Oh, yes." Olive was certain. "It's waiting, all right. You see, I know the *real* story. I know what makes it howl so pitifully, poor creature. It won't rest. It simply won't rest," she repeated mysteriously. "Not until he comes back."

"Who?" Mandy prompted, her eyes wide. Goose bumps were prickling her arms and the back of her neck.

But Olive trailed off and her head began to nod. Her eyelids drooped again. The sound of gentle snoring filled the room.

"Oh, Nana." Hayley looked at Mandy and James apologetically and shrugged her shoulders. "Sorry," she whispered. "She does this. Just goes off."

Mandy tried to hide her disappointment. There were so many questions that she wanted answered. The memory of the sorrowful howling she'd heard in the middle of that inky black night in the tent was with her still. It was an anguished cry. She shivered. She'd give anything to be able to find the dog and bring it comfort.

"We've tired your nana out," James remarked.

"Just as well." Hayley sprang up. "Nana can go on for hours, given half the chance. And I want to go and check on the kittens. Coming?"

Mandy exchanged glances with James, who nodded. They stood up.

"Coming," she said, following Hayley out of the room.

*   *   *

"Perfect timing," James announced, spotting Drs. Adam and Emily on the terrace.

"Ready to go back to the camp?" Dr. Emily asked.

"Yes, thanks." Mandy sighed.

"The mother cat has joined her kittens in the box," Dr. Adam told Hayley.

"Come back and see the kittens before you leave, OK?" Hayley grinned.

"We will," said Mandy. "I've got to bring your things back, anyway." She took a last look at the bundles of fur in the box. She was always surprised at the perfect pink of the underside of their tiny paws. "Bye, Hayley."

"Bye, Mandy. . . . Bye, James. Bye, Dr. Adam and Dr. Emily."

Mandy and James waved until the Land Rover turned a corner, and Hayley and The Grubby Duck were out of sight.

In the front passenger seat, Dr. Emily had a map spread across her knees. "Dad and I are going to take a different route across Dalton Heath back to our camp," she told Mandy and James. "There are some gorgeous places to see."

"And here comes the rain!" Dr. Adam announced as the first big drops began to fall. "So it's just as well that we're not walking."

In the back of the car, James yawned. The steady motion and the hum of the engine made Mandy feel sleepy, too, but she was determined not to miss the views from the window. She noticed that the bank of angry-looking clouds and pelting rain was smudging the lines of the smooth horizon along the edge of the heath. It seemed that the lovely colors of the landscape were running together like ink in water.

"But it *can't* rain on our vacation!" Dr. Emily groaned. The sky grew darker as the rain worsened, and Mandy's father switched on the car's headlights. There was a forked flash of lightning that lit up the threatening clouds ahead of them.

"Wow," said Mandy, her ears tuned for the crack of thunder to follow. The wipers on the windshield swiped at the furious rain, but they could barely cope with the volume of water.

"It's a cloudburst," James said knowledgeably as the thunder boomed over the moor.

"I think I'll have to pull over because —" Dr. Adam began, but he didn't finish his sentence.

Dr. Emily's sudden scream made Mandy's heart lurch painfully against her ribs. "Watch out, Adam! Look *out!*"

Seven

Mandy was thrown against the strap of her seat belt as Dr. Adam jammed his foot hard on the brakes of the Land Rover. The car swerved to a stop with a spine-chilling squeal from the protesting tires.

"Oh!" Mandy cried, shocked. "What is it? What happened?"

"A *man*!" Dr. Adam was breathing hard. "Where did he come from? He stepped right out in front of me!"

"Are you all right?" Dr. Emily had unbuckled her seat belt and turned to check on Mandy and James. Blackie was clambering back up onto the seat between them. He had been thrown into the space between the front seats when the car had braked. Dr. Emily stroked the dog gently to calm him.

"Fine," James mumbled, groping around on the floor. "Only, I lost my glasses."

"Oh, James, sorry," Dr. Emily said.

"I'm OK," Mandy said, reaching down to help her friend. "Here they are, James — not broken or anything."

"Stay in the car," Dr. Adam instructed. "I'll take a look around." He got out and pulled the waterproof hood of his jacket over his head. The rain lashed down, drumming on the roof of the car.

"He gave me a terrible fright." Dr. Emily breathed, her hand over her heart. "One minute, the road was clear, and the next, this figure just loomed up out of the rain. Where *could* he have come from all of a sudden?"

"Somebody out walking, I expect," James said, his arm around his dog.

"In this awful weather?" Mandy asked. "He must be crazy."

The car door opened and her father leaped into his seat. "Ugh!" he said. "It's coming down in buckets!"

"Any sign of him?" Dr. Emily asked anxiously.

"No." Her husband frowned. "I can't see a soul. It's a miracle I didn't hit him. Now he seems to have vanished."

"Let's go back a little," Dr. Emily suggested. "He

might be walking toward Dalton. We could see if he's OK and offer him a lift."

"All right." Dr. Adam put the Land Rover into reverse, and moved off slowly, backward. Mandy craned her neck to see if she could spot the man, though she couldn't see much of anything in the driving rain.

"No, he's disappeared," Dr. Adam declared after a while, looking around him. "How odd."

"He might have reached The Grubby Duck by now," James said cheerfully.

"Well, let's hope he's all right, wherever he is," Dr. Emily said, smoothing out the creases in the map. "We'd better get going, Adam. I need a hot drink!"

"Me, too," said Mandy, looking out of the window as the Land Rover began to pull off.

And then she saw it. It was lying on the road, mud-splattered and soggy with rain, its drawstring loops trailing. It was the cloth bag that belonged to the man they'd met on the heath. Mandy reached across Blackie and nudged James. She pointed as they sped away.

James raised himself in his seat and looked out. "Oh! That's —" he began, his eyebrows raised.

"Shhh!" Mandy warned, putting her finger to her lips. She knew that her parents wouldn't be pleased to find out that she had befriended a stranger on the moor.

"What did you say, James?" Dr. Emily was rubbing at

the misty inside of the windshield. James looked at Mandy, who shook her head.

"Nothing," murmured James. "I was just saying to Mandy that I wish I'd brought a snorkel!"

Dr. Emily laughed. "Oh, James! It's not that bad. It'll pass soon. I bet tomorrow will be a lovely sunny day."

"I hope so." Mandy sighed.

"Me, too." Dr. Adam smiled. "I feel calmer now. That man gave me a tremendous shock. Let's head for the camp and that hot drink!"

It wasn't long before the oil lamps were glowing at strategic points around the camp. As night pressed in on them — made darker still by the thick band of heavy clouds — Mandy was struck again by the wildness of the huge, empty landscape around her. But, with the flickering of the fire in their midst, and the circle of hissing lamps burning bright, it felt cozy just the same.

"Good thing these are called hurricane lamps," James remarked as the flame inside the glass flickered and leaped in the wind. He opened a big tin of dog food for Blackie, who ate as though he hadn't in days. Then, keeping a safe distance from the fire, the Labrador lazily scratched an ear.

"Is everyone game for a hike tomorrow toward the River Esk — weather permitting?" Dr. Adam asked.

Mandy nodded. "I am."

"Me, too," James added.

Dr. Emily opened the palm of her hand as the rain began again. "Oh . . . this *is* annoying," she said. "I was hoping for a game of cards this evening, under the stars."

"Quick, let's clean up before the heavens open again," Dr. Adam urged. Everyone began to scurry around, collecting the mugs and dinner plates. The fire hissed and spluttered as the rain quickened.

"It's relentless," said Dr. Emily.

"Take cover!" James yelled, diving into the tent with Blackie hot on his heels.

"Ugh! Wet dog — and on *my* sleeping bag, too," Mandy scolded playfully.

"I'm glad it's raining." James grinned. "It got us out of a long session of cards — and your dad always wins, anyway! Now we can talk."

"Mandy?" Dr. Emily called from her tent. "When this rain eases off a little, you and James should take a shower, OK?"

James wrinkled his nose at Mandy, and she burst into giggles.

"Shh!" James frowned.

She poked her head out. "OK, Mom," she yelled. Then

she spun around to face James. "The *bag!* It looked just like the one belonging to that strange man!"

James agreed. "So it must have been *him* wandering across the road in front of your dad's car."

"Poor man," Mandy said. "Still out searching for his dog, even in this terrible weather."

"Why doesn't he go off and check at the police station and the SPCA," James wondered out loud.

"Perhaps he'll try there tomorrow," Mandy suggested as she busied herself trying to make the available space in the tent comfortable. Their ground cloth was smeared with mud, and Blackie's blanket was damp. She straightened out the sleeping bags and neatened their pile of belongings as best she could. James amused himself by making patterns on the sloping sides of the tent with his flashlight. It was silent, except for the pitter-patter of the rain and the whoosh of the trees in the wind.

"I wonder if we'll hear it tonight," Mandy whispered, hugging her knees.

James threw back his head and howled — a terrifying, thin wail that made Blackie sit up and cock his head. Mandy threw a pillow at her friend.

"Calm down," growled Dr. Adam from the other tent.

"Sorry, Dr. Adam," said James, trying not to laugh.

"Be serious," Mandy whispered urgently. The wind

plucked at the ropes of the tent, and it shuddered. Blackie turned circles on his blanket, then curled up on it, putting his head on his paws with a big sigh. "Listen to that wind. I hate to think of any poor animal roaming around on a night like this one," said Mandy.

"I wish Hayley's nana hadn't fallen asleep like that," James admitted crossly.

"Olive," Mandy reminded him. "We didn't find out very much about the legend, did we? We don't even know what sort of dog it is." Mandy smoothed Blackie's soft ears.

They talked about the moor and the man on the bench, and then James remembered some ghost stories he'd heard at school. He told them in a deep rumbling voice, which made Mandy weak from laughter.

"You're supposed to be scared!" James grumbled.

"Nothing scares me!" Mandy giggled. "You should know that by now."

After a while, Mandy noticed that the noise of the rain on the tent had stopped. She looked out. Their Land Rover was sitting in a giant puddle. A thin spiral of steam rose sadly from the embers of their fire.

"Should we brave the showers?" she asked James. "It's not quite dark, and we can take the flashlight."

"Spiders," said James meaningfully. "Anyway, who wants to be clean on a camping trip? Not me!"

Dodging the muddy pools left by the rain, Mandy went across to her parents' tent. It was silent. She opened the flap quietly and peeked in. Her mother and father were fast asleep! She chuckled and turned back, deciding to forget about taking a shower and to suggest a game of Scrabble instead.

And then she froze.

The eerie howl came echoing across the moor, reaching Mandy loud and clear. There was no mistaking it. She was not imagining it. And there it was again!

"*James!*" Mandy threw herself into the tent to find James sitting bolt upright, his eyes as round as saucers. Blackie was sitting up beside him.

"I heard it!" he stuttered. "This time, I really did hear it. The howl!"

"It's not a fox, is it?" Mandy demanded.

Slowly, James shook his head. "No, it's not."

For a few seconds, they looked at each other, with their ears straining and their thoughts racing.

"Should we go and take a look?" Mandy whispered at last. Her heart was pounding with anticipation. "It *might* be Rover . . . wouldn't it be wonderful if we could find the dog and then take it back to its owner?"

"Yes," James agreed. "It really would. The poor man seemed so sad — but what about your mom and dad?" he asked.

"Asleep," Mandy whispered. Her heart was thundering against her rib cage. She was thrilled by the thought of trying to find the dog but terrified just the same. It seemed a dangerous mission but a worthwhile one. The thought of the young man gave her courage.

"Come on, James! Quickly!"

James put on his shoes and his waterproof jacket. "Let's go, then. Get your coat. I'll bring the flashlight."

They tried to persuade Blackie to remain behind in the tent. Using a masterful tone, James commanded the Labrador to stay.

"Quiet, James!" Mandy warned. "We don't want to wake my mom and dad!"

Blackie looked puzzled. He sat down, wagging his tail feebly as the tent was secured by the ties at the opening. Then he eased his shiny black nose through the flap. Mandy burst into giggles.

"Shhh!" James warned her and tried again. "*Stay*, Blackie!" Blackie withdrew his nose and whimpered.

"That did it," James said smugly. "Let's go."

The rain stopped, but the moor was now plunged into darkness. There was no sign of a moon and even the stars were hidden by heavy clouds. They walked side by side using the flashlight, which cast a circular beam of cheery yellow on the soggy ground.

James stopped next to the Land Rover. "Which way?" he whispered.

As if guiding them, the wavering howl rose again. It was a thin, mournful sound, piercing the still of the night like a knife. Mandy wasn't afraid, but it gave her goose bumps nevertheless. Her arms prickled and she rubbed them.

"I thought you said that nothing ever scared you," James teased as they turned in the direction of the howl.

"That's right," said Mandy. "I'm not scared, I'm just . . . oh!" She gasped and clutched at James in sudden terror as a dark shape came crashing through the undergrowth straight toward them.

"What!" James grabbed at Mandy in panic, then she felt his grip relax. "*Blackie!* You nearly scared us to death! I thought I'd told you to stay."

Mandy felt Blackie's apologetic tail thumping against her leg. "He might be scared," she suggested. "He doesn't much like the strange noises of the night — do you, boy?"

"OK, you can come." James gave in, patting Blackie. "But it's wet and muddy out here, and you're going to get filthy."

"So are we," Mandy reasoned.

Blackie fell into step beside James, walking to heel

instead of bounding ahead the way he usually did. Mandy had never known him so obedient — or could he really be scared?

In the chilly night air, Mandy linked her arm through James's. They pressed on, moving steadily toward the sound of the howl. Once or twice Mandy stumbled. Then James paused to look back at the Land Rover.

"I'm getting my bearings," he announced. "The last thing we need to do is to get lost. Remember that tree there — with the split trunk. OK?"

"OK," said Mandy, feeling for Blackie's smooth head. The dog was clearly agitated, pausing to lift his front paw whenever the howl sliced through the night, his body taut. Thick cushions of mud were sticking to the bottom of her boots, smearing their way up the lower half of her pant legs.

Mandy was starting to think that they were venturing too far from camp, when James suddenly gasped.

"Look! Mandy!"

Ahead of them, they could see the blackened, ruined walls of a small building. Ivy-covered and broken, the toppled stones lay in heaps across the old foundation. Only the remains of a door frame stood upright, still fixed to the floor. Dried leaves rustled in a swirl of wind and rose spookily, before settling with a sigh.

James swiveled the flashlight, picking out the cavernous mouth of an ancient fireplace. "It's in ruins," he whispered in awe. "It must be ages since anyone lived here."

A fierce gust of wind rushed at the house, and the door frame swayed and groaned under the onslaught. There was the sound of frantically fluttering wings. A hundred or more flapping creatures erupted from the crumbling walls of the cottage. They burst up into the night sky, giving off a high, thin wail as they swooped and dived for cover.

Mandy gasped and cowered in shock.

"Bats!" said James, who had ducked his head and was keeping it low. "We must have disturbed a whole colony of them!"

Mandy breathed a sigh of relief and stood up again. Her legs still felt shaky.

The ruin was deserted — and the howling seemed to have stopped. Blackie stood between them, as close as he could get to the reassuring safety of the people he loved. His ears were lying flat on his head, and his tail was tucked tightly between his legs.

"It's stopped," James whispered, his voice strained with nerves. "Look, we'd better turn back."

Suddenly, the bruised darkness of the night was split open by a flash of white light. It was a great flash of lightning, illuminating the moor and the ruined house.

Mandy clutched again at James and in that terrifying second, standing among the ruins, they saw it.

It was the creature that everyone had told them about.

Into the arc of light cast by James's trembling flashlight beam, stepped a thin and elegant greyhound.

Mandy's eyes widened in surprise. The dog was the palest gray — almost white. On its sculptured face was the saddest expression Mandy had ever seen. "Oh, James!" she murmured. "Poor dog!"

Mandy felt that James was squeezing her arm a little

harder than he intended. His eyes were fixed on the dog. Blackie had dropped back, his head drooping. And, as they watched, the greyhound in the ruins lifted its head and howled. It was a bloodcurdling moan that sent shivers running down Mandy's back to the very base of her spine.

James jumped. "What do we do now?" he asked, raising his voice above the noise of the wind. A clap of thunder rolled overhead, echoing across the enormous moor.

She looked at him, then back at the dog, almost expecting it to disappear as magically as it had arrived — noiseless as smoke. "Do you think this *could* be Rover?"

He nodded. "Maybe. The poor thing must've been taking shelter up here. The dog's wearing a collar — let's see what it says."

They edged nearer, moving slowly so as not to startle the proud creature in the ruins. But the dog looked back at them steadily. It made no attempt to investigate the arrival of the strangers, or to run away. It simply stared, its big eyes unblinking. James focused the beam of his flashlight on the loose collar around the dog's thin neck. Its name had been painted there in large luminous letters, plain for James and Mandy to see. ROVER.

"It's him!" Mandy cried excitedly. "It *is* Rover."

"Thank goodness," James said. "We've found him."

"We should take him back to our camp," Mandy whispered. "He might need food and water."

"We'll have to catch him first," James said.

Mandy took a step forward. "Hello," she spoke soothingly. "Come here . . . come and say hello." The dog was still, its regal head held high. It looked directly at Mandy, then looked away, lifted its head to the sky and howled.

"Oooh!" said James, covering his ears. "I hate that sound."

"Here," Mandy crouched low and put out a hand. "We won't hurt you, boy. Come here."

"This is odd," James decided. "I mean, it doesn't seem particularly frightened of us, or even pleased to see us. It's as though Rover *expected* us to be strolling past in the middle of the night! He's taking no notice of us at all."

"He doesn't seem to want to leave the ruins of that house, that's for sure," Mandy said. Then, she had a sudden thought. She rummaged in the pocket of her coat.

"Here," she said. "I've got some candy in my pocket." Mandy tossed a piece toward the dog. It fell with a tiny thud, then rolled. The greyhound's eyes followed the candy until it came to rest a short distance from where the dog was standing. But Rover made no attempt to go over and investigate.

"Hmm," said James, perplexed. "Obviously not hungry." He shivered.

"It's cold," Mandy said. "Let's try walking away. Maybe the dog will follow us."

"OK," James agreed readily. But Blackie was as still as a statue, staring at the greyhound as if he couldn't believe his eyes. "Don't be silly," James told him, "it's only a dog!"

Mandy called again to the greyhound as they walked away, glancing over her shoulder to see if he had moved. "Rover! Come here!" But the dog remained rooted to the floor, looking ahead. The greyhound gave another quavering howl.

"Should we go and get your mom and dad?" James suggested. "They'd know what to do."

"No," Mandy said after a bit. "No, I don't think they'd be happy to know that we sneaked off without saying we were going."

"It *is* very dark — and late." James shined the flashlight on his watch and yawned.

"The dog isn't going to follow us," Mandy decided. "I think we might have to give up for now. We'll have to make some sort of a plan. And quickly."

James nodded. They were some distance away from the ruin now. Blackie kept tight to James's side, pressing close up against him. "It's all right, boy," James said warmly. "We're going back to the camp. Come on."

They set off in silence, back the way they had come. The ground made sucking noises underfoot. Mandy was relieved when the wind pushed aside a strip of low clouds to reveal a brilliantly starry sky — only to cover it up again seconds later.

"Hold up," said James, stopping. "Are we going in the right direction?"

"I think so," Mandy replied vaguely. She simply wasn't sure. She and James had been so eager to find the source of the howling, they hadn't been as careful as they should have been.

"Footprints," said James, swinging the flashlight around at their feet. "We must have left our prints in the mud. But where are they?" The blot of yellow light danced ahead, and Blackie whined.

And then the flashlight went out. It was so sudden that Mandy gasped. The intense, velvety darkness enveloped them as though someone had thrown a blanket over their heads.

"Oh, no," James said, in a very small voice. "The battery's dead."

"Oh . . . James, no!" Mandy whispered. "What are we going to do now?"

Eight

"Don't panic," James said. "We can't be far from the tent."

Taking a deep, calming breath, Mandy tried to figure out where they were. But the sky was inky black, without even a star to light their way. Featureless moor stretched away from them in every direction. She linked her arm through James's, and they slowly moved forward together. Confused by the darkness and sensing their fear, Blackie whimpered and pushed his cold nose into the palm of Mandy's hand.

"It's OK, Blackie," she said more brightly than she

was feeling. Then she added, "Mom and Dad are going to be very upset if we're not in our tent in the morning."

"We'll be there," said James, walking straight into a thornbush.

"Ow!" gasped Mandy as a little branch smacked her in the face.

"Blackie?" James commanded hopefully. "Home, boy! Take us home!" The Labrador swirled eagerly around their feet. They could hear his tail swish from side to side. He seemed relieved to be away from the burned-out house.

"Home!" Mandy tried in vain. Blackie hadn't a clue what he was supposed to do, she could tell, though he seemed eager to try to please.

"Well." Mandy sighed. "What now? Which way?"

Just then, the clouds moved slightly and a sliver of moonlight shone down onto the moor. And there, standing in the moonlight, was Rover.

Mandy and James gasped in astonishment.

The slim, pale shape was moving up ahead of them. Mandy could just make out the outline of his curved back and the curl of his long tail.

"Is Rover following us or are we following him, I wonder?" James whispered.

"I'm sure we *should* follow him!" Mandy was excited. "He's out of the house and heading that way — come on!"

Clutching on to each other, they hurried forward, trying to close the gap between themselves and Rover's shadowy outline. From time to time, the graceful dog stopped and briefly waited before moving on. He slipped across the moor like a cloud chased by the wind. Blackie had dropped back, and James had to keep urging him to keep up.

"Blackie's normally such a friendly dog," James grumbled. "What's that word for having a fear of wide-open spaces?"

"Agoraphobia," Mandy said.

"Well, I think Blackie's got it." James chuckled. "At least, he's had it ever since we've been on this moor!"

Stumbling along in the dark, Mandy realized that she had complete trust in the strange animal up ahead. The way the dog kept stopping, checking to see if they were keeping up, made her feel safe. She felt grateful and wished that it would allow them to pet it. But Rover seemed determined not to come too close to the strangers on the moor.

"What if this dog isn't Rover at all?" said James. "I mean, we might be following the animal to goodness knows where."

"Don't, James," Mandy said. "I'm sure he's leading us back to the camp. Let's just believe in him because . . . there! See — there's Dad's Land Rover!" The bulky shape of the car loomed out of the darkness in the clearing up ahead. Blackie darted away and slipped hurriedly through the tent flap. Mandy laughed with relief.

"Shhh!" James whispered. "We don't want to be discovered now."

"We were so close — so close, after all! We shouldn't have been worried," Mandy spoke softly.

"And what if we had gone in the opposite direction and fallen into one of those squishy, smelly bog things?" James demanded.

"All the more reason to be grateful to Rover." Mandy smiled. "Rover!" she called softly. But Rover was already moving away across the moor, back the way they had come. His pale coat shimmered as he slipped away.

"What an amazing dog!" Mandy muttered. "No wonder his owner didn't want to give up on him."

"I wish I had a huge, juicy, meaty bone to give him to say thanks," James whispered, ducking in through the tent opening. "I don't know how we would have made it back without his help."

"Tomorrow," Mandy said with determination, "we'll have to find that man and tell him we've seen the dog up here, near that wreck of a house. OK?"

"Hmm," mumbled James. He was lying, fully dressed, in his muddy boots, and his eyes were already closed.

*   *   *

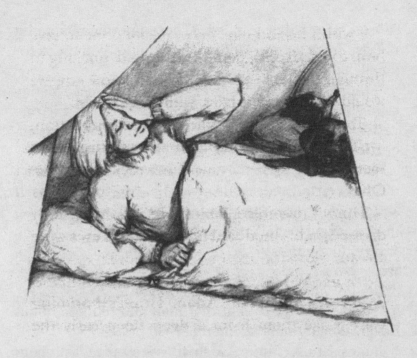

"Wake up, you two!" Dr. Adam's booming voice woke them from a deep sleep early the next morning. James groaned and rolled over. Rubbing her eyes, Mandy sat up, and the memories of the previous night's adventure flooded back.

Dr. Adam's cheery face peeped in through the tent's opening. "Morning all," he said brightly. "Who wants breakfast?" James groaned again.

"Hi, Dad." Mandy smiled blearily. "Did you sleep well?"

"Yes." Her father grinned. "There's nothing like a bit of crisp fresh air and Mother Earth under your back for a really good night's sleep."

"I thought I'd take a shower before breakfast," Mandy said, suddenly remembering that she was still wearing yesterday's clothing. The hems of her jeans were encrusted with dried mud.

"OK, honey. Join us when you're ready." Dr. Adam let the tent flap fall and strode away. Blackie shook himself and yawned. Then he wandered off after Mandy's father, wagging his tail.

Prodding James in the ribs, Mandy hissed, "Wake up. We've got to come up with a plan."

"Plan?" James mumbled. "What plan?"

"We have to try to find that man and tell him about Rover," Mandy said. "Remember?"

James sat up. "Mmm. Gosh, it was strange last night. I feel as if I might have dreamed about that dog."

"It wasn't a dream." Mandy smiled. "Rover was a lovely, amazing dog. He brought us home."

"Yes." James nodded. "Thank goodness."

"I wish we'd thought to ask that man his name — and where he *lived*!" Mandy said, angry with herself. "We must let him know that we've found his dog!"

"We don't know for *sure* that it's his dog," James said.

"It must be!" Mandy cried. "It said Rover on the name tag!"

"Well." James brightened. "Rover's owner might be hanging around near where we first met him. He said he was going to wait for the dog to turn up."

"Well, he's not likely to be sitting there *still*, is he?" Mandy made a face at her friend. "He would be frozen solid by now!"

"I suppose so," James muttered. "He'd be starving, too. I know I am."

"You go and have breakfast, then," Mandy said. "I'm going to take a shower. It'll give us time to think about what we're going to do."

Mandy had the shower to herself. As she washed her hair, she thought about the greyhound and wondered where it had spent the night. She hoped it hadn't been cold, or frightened, and wished she could have found a way to tempt it back to their camp. Then it would have been easy to reunite Rover with his owner the next day.

Mandy dressed quickly, more determined than ever to find the man that she was certain was the dog's owner. But how? And what if the dog was now roaming farther across the moor, never to be found again?

She was troubled as she walked back to camp, her shampoo and dirty clothes tucked under her arm. Her clean hair began to dry in the autumn sunshine.

In their tent, James was examining a map. "It shows all of the moor," he told her excitedly. "I asked your dad if I could see it."

"Oh?" said Mandy, interested. She sat down beside him on his sleeping bag.

"Look here," James began, pushing his glasses up on his nose. "You won't believe it." James stabbed a finger at the map. "We're here, right?"

"Right," said Mandy, looking at the map. "So?"

"Remember that big white cross we saw on the moor — MacArthur's Point?"

"Yes." Mandy frowned.

"Well, here it is — it's not very far away from us at all. It's just a bit over to the west, in a straight line! I told you we could have walked back to the camp from where we spotted the man!"

"You mean," Mandy said slowly, "that it's really close?"

"Yes!" James replied. "See? We could easily get back to the bench where we met the man, just by walking this way."

"James, that's great!" Mandy said. "We'll go later, just as soon as we can."

There was a rustling at the tent opening and Dr. Emily looked in. Her long red hair swung over her shoulders. "Hello." She smiled. "Did you sleep well?"

"Yes, thanks, Mom."

"Do you want any breakfast? I can't keep things warm much longer," Dr. Emily said.

"Coming." Mandy sprang up.

"We were looking at Dr. Adam's map of the moor," James told her as they squeezed out of the tent.

"Huge, isn't it?" Dr. Emily remarked. "Mandy's dad is hoping to catch our supper in the River Esk today. Do you like to fish, James?"

James looked at Mandy. "Um, yes. I'll give it a try," he said.

"Good. We're going to pop into town to pick up a few things we need first. Bait, for one thing!" Dr. Emily handed James a plate piled high with crispy bacon and toast. Blackie sidled closer, his nose twitching at the delicious smell.

"I've fed Blackie," Dr. Emily added. "He was ravenous. Anyone would think he'd been up all night chasing rabbits or something!"

Mandy exchanged glances with James as she spread strawberry jam on her toast. "It must be all this fresh air." She smiled. "I'm ravenous, too."

*   *   *

After breakfast, Mandy was desperate to dash across the moor to MacArthur's Point. But she discovered that there wasn't a moment to spare. Dr. Adam was eager to set off on their fishing trip. James was on cleanup duty, and Mandy had to help her mother shake out the sleeping bags and tidy up the tents. Dr. Adam was loading up the Land Rover with the picnic lunch, the fishing rods, wading boots, and other items when he heard the thud of boots and looked up.

"Just passing by, doing my rounds," said a smiling man in a uniform. "Everything all right up here?"

"Fine, thanks," said Dr. Adam. "Lovely day, isn't it?"

"Great," said the ranger. "I'm glad the rain has moved on. By the way, let me know if you need any more kerosene for your lamps — I've got some."

"Thanks, but we're fine," Dr. Adam said.

"Well, then, I'll be on my way. Good day to you."

"Bye," called Dr. Adam. He went back to packing up the car. Mandy waited until the ranger was a few yards away from their camp, then ran after him.

"Excuse me," she called.

"Yes?" He smiled and stood looking down at her with both hands on his hips. "How can I help you?"

"Um, I was just wondering . . . do you happen to know a man who owns a greyhound?"

The ranger looked thoughtful. "Has this man got a name?" he asked, pulling on his beard.

"That's just it, you see," Mandy explained. "We don't know his name."

"And where exactly might he live?" the ranger probed.

"I don't know that, either," Mandy admitted. "But I do know that he's about eighteen years old and he's got a curved scar on his cheek. He owns a dog called Rover, which I *think* is a greyhound."

The ranger raised his eyebrows and looked thoughtful.

"Do you know him?" Mandy prompted.

"I can't say that I do." The ranger shook his head. "I know most people who live around these parts, but I don't know the man you're looking for — of that, I am certain."

"Oh, well . . . I'm sorry to have troubled you," Mandy said politely.

"Mandy!" Dr. Adam beckoned. "Let's get going!"

"Perhaps he was from out of town?" the ranger added kindly.

"Perhaps," Mandy said. "Thanks, anyway." She turned and hurried back to where Dr. Adam was revving the engine of the Land Rover.

Mandy couldn't bear to think of Rover having to spend one more night alone on the moor. The crumbling walls of the old ruin didn't give much shelter from the weather. What if there was another storm tonight? She would have to do something — anything — to reunite the dog with his owner.

Nine

With the market stalls dismantled, Dalton looked very different. Now that the streets were almost empty of people and stalls, Mandy could see how small Dalton really was.

"Somebody here *must* know the man," she managed to whisper to James as her father eased the Land Rover into a parking space.

"The ranger didn't," James replied. "And maybe he was right. Maybe Rover's owner was just passing through."

Mandy wished with all her heart that they could find him and return his lovely greyhound. Then she could put it out of her mind and really enjoy the day at the river.

"Well," she said, "if we can't find the man, we'll just have to find Rover. We can't just leave him wandering. He needs rescuing. He needs *us*."

"You're right," James agreed quietly. "We may have to ask your mom and dad for help — even if it means telling them about last night."

Dr. Emily turned to James. "I'm sure Dr. Adam could do with some help finding some bait. I want to get a loaf of bread and a few apples. Do you want to come with me, Mandy?"

"I know where the village store is, Mom," Mandy said. "I'll meet you there in a few minutes. There's something I want to do first. Is that OK?"

"Don't hold us up, Mandy," Dr. Adam said. "It's such a great day. We don't want to waste it."

"I won't, Dad," Mandy promised.

"OK," said James, putting on Blackie's leash. "See you later." He shrugged his shoulders at Mandy and she winked at him.

Mandy had a plan. There was one person in Dalton who just might be able to help her — Nicholas Moon. The old man had said that he'd lived in Dalton all of his life. This time, Mandy vowed, she would not irritate him by mentioning the legend of the moor. As she pushed open the door to the store, she found herself hoping that Mr. Moon would welcome her with a smile.

"Good morning," he began, standing up so hastily that he overturned his stool. "How may I — oh, it's *you*. You're still in town?" He took off his glasses and began to polish them on his jacket.

"Hello, Mr. Moon," Mandy said, smiling.

"Did you change your mind about that book?" He scowled at her, but she thought she could see a friendly twinkle in his eye.

"I haven't come about a book," she replied boldly. "I've come about a *man* who might live locally. I thought you might know him."

"What's his name?" Mr. Moon looked at her through his glasses. He didn't seem very interested.

"I'm afraid that I don't know," Mandy said. "My friend James and I met him out on the heath. He'd lost his dog — a greyhound. We think we've found the dog. . . ." She trailed off. Mr. Moon had folded his arms.

"What does the man look like?" he probed.

"Pale skin, young . . . um, very short hair — and he's got a long, curved scar on his cheek. Do you know him?" Mandy felt like a detective. She was really proud of her full description. Surely Mr. Moon would recognize him?

"He's not from Dalton; that I can tell you." Mr. Moon

was certain. "I would know anyone answering to that description — and I don't."

"Oh." Mandy was bitterly disappointed. The ranger must have been right. She looked around the creepy little store, breathing in the dank smell of the place, like old flowers left too long in a vase.

The old man softened. "I'm sorry I can't help. Have you tried the police station?"

"Oh, no! Thank you," Mandy said. "I don't think I'll need to do that."

"Take the animal to the local shelter, that's my advice," Mr. Moon said, nodding. "You don't want a dog roaming the streets, rummaging through garbage pails and . . ."

"Thank you for your help." Mandy smiled, cutting in quickly, and hoping she wasn't being rude. "I'm in a bit of a hurry, so . . ."

"Wait a moment," said Mr. Moon. "Here's something to help you remember your trip to Dalton — a gift."

Mandy looked at the small book that he'd thrust into her hands. "*A Pictorial History of Dalton*," she read. "Thank you very much. Good-bye, Mr. Moon." Mandy was soon out of the door and dashing along the cobbled street to the corner store, where her mother was just shutting the door behind her.

Mandy sighed to herself as she pushed the book into her pocket. She realized that finding the greyhound's owner might not be as easy as she'd thought. They wouldn't have a chance to see if the man was waiting at the bench until tomorrow.

In the meantime, Rover might still be wandering the moor. Whatever happened, they couldn't leave him for another night. He would soon start to weaken and die.

"Are you OK?" Dr. Emily smoothed Mandy's hair.

"Yes," said Mandy.

"Then wipe that worried frown off your face, and let's get down to the river!" Dr. Emily said with a smile.

After a picnic lunch, they walked for several miles across the moors, following the signposted bridle paths uphill and down through the dappled dales, until Dr. Emily declared that she couldn't walk another step. Blackie raced around, splashing in and out of the river and cooling everyone down with showers of droplets each time he shook himself!

Each step of the way, Mandy had kept her eyes peeled for Rover. She hoped for a glimpse of his pale coat or his proud head, but she was disappointed.

The sun was sinking in a cloudless sky by the time they arrived back at their camp. Mandy was relieved to get out of the car. It smelled strongly of the fish that James and her father had caught late that afternoon — a large trout each!

Supper was fun, and Mandy laughed at the delight with which James dissected and ate his trout.

"Wow!" he kept saying, his mouth full. "This is really good. Try some, Mandy."

"No, thanks," said Mandy, laughing, before sinking her teeth into a juicy veggie burger. She was anxious for the meal to be over. She was eager for a chance to look for Rover. She crossed her fingers under the table. *Please, let us find him. Please!*

"Do you feel like a walk?" James asked suddenly when they'd cleared the plates. Blackie cocked his head with interest, then jumped up and wagged his tail.

"Not me!" Dr. Adam said from the depths of a canvas chair. "I plan to sit here and enjoy the sunset. Thank goodness the rain has moved on."

"Another walk?" Dr. Emily groaned. "But we've walked *miles* today."

"Oh, yes!" Mandy grinned at James. "Is that all right with you, Blackie?" The Labrador barked obligingly and turned in a circle of excitement. "Please, Mom, can we?"

"You won't get lost, will you?" Mandy's mother said, dunking the plates into a washbowl.

"We'll take Dr. Adam's map," James assured her.

"And remember to watch out for bogs," Dr. Adam cautioned. "I don't like the idea of plucking you out of one."

"We'll be careful." Mandy laughed. "See you later."

As James and Mandy raced back to their tent for the map, Dr. Adam called after them. "Make sure you're back before it gets dark!"

Light from the sinking sun had turned the heather a honey-gold in color. The moorland was hemmed in on one side by a craggy cliff, and on the other by a spread of dense forest. As they set out, Mandy felt hopeful. This time, the wind, the intense dark, and the mud could not hamper them.

"Just as well you suggested this walk," she said. "I couldn't have waited until tomorrow. I keep thinking that poor Rover might be moving farther and farther away from us with every passing minute. And he must be *so* hungry."

"If we're lucky, he may be attracted by the smell of food from the camp," James said. He paused, and opened out the map, turning it this way and that.

"There's MacArthur's Point," said Mandy, pointing to the cross on the map. "Let's go."

Blackie trotted along beside them. He seemed relaxed and content and showing none of the signs of his earlier, nervous behavior. To the west, the sun dipped behind the trees, and a long, cool shadow embraced the moor.

Mandy shivered. "There goes the sun. It'll be dark soon. We mustn't be long or my parents will come searching for us. Dad'll be furious."

"Well, hurry up, then," James urged. "Let's look for that man first — if we find him, he can help us to search for Rover. If he isn't there, we can just go back in a loop past the burned-out cottage and see if the dog is still there."

They began to jog, to Blackie's evident delight. He loped along with them, his ears flapping. After five minutes, Mandy was tired. A small stone had found its way into her sneaker and was rubbing painfully against her heel. She loosened her laces and eased it out with her finger.

"Look!" James shouted. "There's the cross! I told you it wasn't far."

The big cross loomed out of the gloom of dusk. Beyond it was the bench where the man had been sitting. It was deserted.

"He's not there!" Mandy sighed.

"Hmm," said James, pushing his hair out of his eyes. "It looks like he's moved on. He must have given up on finding his dog. Well, let's rescue Rover, if we can. Come on, Mandy, it's this way."

"Wait!" Mandy reached out and grasped James's sleeve.

Someone was waving to them from behind a group of trees. Mandy narrowed her eyes. Was she imagining things? The gathering darkness must be playing tricks on her.

But Blackie had seen something, too. He dropped like a stone, his ears flat back on his head and his hackles bristling.

"Someone's waving to us," she said. Her heart began to race.

"Where?" James followed her gaze. "Wow . . . someone *is* waving — and they're coming this way," James agreed. He groped in his pocket for the flashlight.

The beam of light made Mandy feel braver. It was creepy being out in the middle of the moor, plunged into the deepening shadows of approaching night. Her heart began to race.

Her voice was faint with nerves, so instead she gave a hearty wave, hoping to show the approaching figure that they were friendly.

"I'll bet it's that ranger who we saw earlier, remember?" James whispered, rather hopefully.

The figure came closer and, suddenly, Mandy knew that it was the strange man they'd seen on the moor the day before. She recognized his suspenders, glinting in the half-light, and his funny boots. Behind him, he trailed his muddy drawstring bag.

"James!" Mandy said excitedly. "It's him! We've found him!"

"Great!" James said.

"Hello," Mandy called again, relaxing. "It's us — Mandy and James. We met on the moor. I think we've seen your dog!"

"We've been trying to find you," James offered.

The man was smiling gently when he reached them. "Hello," he said. "I remember you."

Mandy thought again that he seemed sick. He was so pale that his skin reminded her of rice paper. She wondered if he had eaten since they had last seen him, and how he had managed to stay so clean if he spent the time wandering the muddy moor in search of his dog.

Her hammering heart began to beat more regularly. "We saw Rover!" she told him again.

"He's taken shelter in an old, ruined house," James added.

The man was gazing around at the darkening moor. Instead of whooping for joy, the news did not seem to make an impression on him at all.

Mandy looked at James, puzzled, and he raised his eyebrows at her. Seconds passed in silence.

"Excuse me?" Mandy tried again. "We found your dog."

He turned around, and then blinked at her. Slowly, his

troubled face lit up with joy. "Rover?" he asked, his voice shaking. "*My* Rover? My beautiful greyhound?"

"Yes! Yes!" Mandy answered. "That's what we've been trying to tell you! We're almost sure it was Rover. We're hoping he's still there, in an old house we found."

"Take me to where you saw him, please!" the young man begged.

"OK," said James. "Of course we will. Follow us." He looked around for Blackie. The Labrador was lying a short distance away, his head on his paws. But his eyes were riveted on the young man. "Come here, boy," James urged, striding away. "He's a friend!"

The man followed Mandy and James, though he only spoke a little, not even answering when Mandy asked him a direct question. She decided he was simply very shy, and felt even more sorry for him. He was a loner, a strange, private sort of person who probably had few friends. That was why, she reasoned, he was so devoted to his dog.

"We wondered what your name is," she said brightly, "and where you live. We didn't think we would find you again."

There was silence. James coughed and looked back for his dog. Blackie was following at a distance, his tail tucked between his legs, looking wary.

The man smiled. "I'm William," he said.

"Here we are!" James threw the light of the flashlight at the ruin up ahead. "This is the place where we came across Rover. He was just there, up on the floor of . . ."

William took a step forward, as though in a trance. He stretched his arms out to the walls of the crumbling house. He ran his fingertips lightly over the chunks of blackened stone, carefully fingering the charred remains.

Mandy looked at James and wrinkled her nose. "What *is* he doing?" she whispered.

"Search me." James shrugged. "I told you he was crazy."

The young man seemed lost in a world of his own. He gazed dreamily at the ruins, as if he saw more than blackened bricks. "Thank you, both of you," he said, turning. "You've helped me more than you'll ever know."

With that, he began to rummage in the bag he carried. When he found what he was looking for, he reached for James's hand and pressed something into it. It was cold and hard.

James opened his palm. "It's a watch!" he said, peering at it in the gloom of the dusk. "A pocket watch. But we haven't found your dog yet. I can't take this."

"Take it. It's to thank you," said William, and he went back to examining the house.

Mandy, ignoring the strange gift William had given to James, bit her bottom lip nervously. William was so happy — but there was no sign of Rover! It was almost dark now — her parents would start to get worried very soon.

"The dog isn't here," she whispered to James, horrified to think how disappointed poor William would be when he realized that his dog had disappeared once more.

James sighed heavily. "What rotten luck," he said.

"William . . ." Mandy began, but she didn't get a chance to finish.

A single, heartfelt howl erupted from within the house. It hung, reverberating in the still night air.

William seemed unaffected by the startling sound.

Mandy raised her eyebrows and looked at James. What was happening? They could hear howling, but Rover was nowhere to be seen. Meanwhile, William gazed at the ruins, as if mesmerized.

Mandy glanced at her watch. They really had to go *now*, or there would be search parties looking for them. She nudged James, but he was staring in amazement at the ruined building. For there, standing on a heap of stones, was Rover.

With tears streaming down his cheeks, William rushed to embrace the greyhound, chanting softly, "Rover! Rover!"

The dog pranced, circling his master in an elegant dance that made Mandy want to cry, too.

"They've really missed each other, haven't they?" whispered James.

"Let's go," Mandy murmured. "Let's leave them together now. We've done what we set out to do."

"OK." James grinned. "I figure we've got about five minutes to make it back to camp before it's *really* dark."

After a few steps, Mandy paused to look back. William had found a place to sit among the debris of the collapsed house. He was hugging the dog as if he'd never let it go.

With a huge leap of happiness, Mandy began to run.

Ten

Blackie was the first to reach the camp. He bounded into the clearing, where Dr. Emily was putting a log on the fire, and skidded to a halt at her side.

"Blackie! You startled me." She soothed him, stroking his heaving sides. "Is somebody chasing you?"

"Only us," James called cheerily. "He's a big baby, Dr. Emily. Scared of his own shadow." James ruffled Blackie's glossy head. He was panting and seemed very relieved to be back on familiar territory. James went to get his water bowl.

"You just came back?" asked Dr. Adam, glancing up at the night sky. "Look at those stars!"

"Lovely," Mandy said happily, falling into a chair. "It was great out on the heath."

"I can't believe we're going home tomorrow," said Dr. Emily.

"And I can't believe that Mandy and James haven't rescued a single animal all vacation." Dr. Adam laughed. "That must be a first!"

Mandy looked at James and winked.

"What about the kittens?" Mandy reminded her parents, with a chuckle.

"Oh, yes . . . the kittens, of course! We'll pop in and say good-bye to Hayley and check on the kittens tomorrow, OK?" Dr. Emily suggested. "And return Hayley's things to her."

"Good idea," said Mandy's father.

James dragged a log closer to the fire and sat down on it. Then he reached into his pocket and fished out William's pocket watch. In the light of the fire's flames, the old silver casing shined brilliantly.

Mandy was at his side in an instant. "It's lovely," she whispered.

"What's that, James?" Dr. Emily sounded curious.

"Found it out on the moor," James mumbled. "It's a watch."

"May I have a look?" Dr. Adam reached out for the heavy oval object, swinging on a loop of delicate silver chain. He examined it in the light of an oil lamp. "It may be valuable," he announced, turning it over in his hand. "It's an antique. Perhaps we ought to give it to the police?"

"Can I see, Dad?" Mandy pressed gently at the delicate clasp and the watch opened. On the inside of the lid was an inscription, but the tiny words were difficult to make out. Mandy squinted to see it, while James looked over her shoulder. The words became clear to them at the same moment.

Mandy drew in her breath sharply. She looked at James, who looked back at her with his mouth hanging open. *For William Johnston. Come home to us safely. 1914.*

"Nineteen-fourteen!" James repeated.

"It must have belonged to his grandfather — or even his great-grandfather," Mandy reasoned quickly. "Our William is a young man."

"Whose father?" Dr. Emily asked, looking puzzled.

"Just a man we met on the moor," James explained.

"Oh." Dr. Emily was preoccupied with a book she was reading. "Well, make sure he gets it back, OK?" she advised.

Suddenly, Mandy remembered something. "We must take it to Olive," she said in a low voice. "She'll be able to tell us about it. Look at the name again."

"The *Johnston* family? William *Johnston* . . . Do you think . . . ?" James mused.

"Yes," Mandy said excitedly, cutting him short. "Maybe Olive could tell us something about our William?"

"You know," James said slowly, "I think you may be right."

And, for the first night since their arrival at Dalton Heath, they slept soundly.

It was midmorning before they were ready to leave. James had misplaced one of his shoes and Dr. Emily discovered a carton of orange juice that had leaked in the cooler. After several trips to the big garbage pails near the showers, Mandy helped her father pour water onto the fire left smoldering from breakfast time.

Blackie got into the Land Rover as it was being packed. He seemed eager to leave.

"Dr. Adam?" James asked. "Is it possible for a dog to suffer from agoraphobia?"

Mandy's father roared with laughter. "I don't think so, James. Why?"

"It's Blackie," James said gloomily. "He's been behaving very strangely since we arrived on this moor."

"Well, judging by his energy and the fun he's had on his walks, I don't think it's agoraphobia that's bothering him. I'll take a look at him for you when we get back to the clinic, OK?" Dr. Adam patted the Labrador's smooth head.

"Thanks," James said, looking at Blackie, who had refused to budge from the backseat of the car.

"He just wants to make sure he's not going to be left behind," Dr. Emily said with a smile.

Drs. Adam and Emily had agreed to let Mandy and James spend time with Hayley and her kittens while they had lunch at The Grubby Duck. Mandy hoped it would be possible to visit Olive, too. She felt certain that the old lady would recognize the silver pocket watch that William had given them so gratefully the night before. She couldn't wait to find out if her suspicions were right.

Now they were ready to go, and Mandy felt a pang of regret. She wished she had had the chance to get to know Rover, the extraordinary greyhound that had led them home — but the dog had been as strange and secretive as his master.

"Good-bye," she and James chorused as they pulled away from their site.

"It's been a lovely vacation," Dr. Emily said. "We must come back again one day."

*   *   *

Hayley Roberts was sitting cross-legged on the terrace of her parents' restaurant. One of the kittens was snuggled in her lap when Mandy and James arrived.

"Oh, hi!" Hayley looked pleased to see them.

"Hello." Mandy smiled. "Gosh, haven't they changed in just a couple of days!" The kittens looked fluffier and fuller and seemed more confident.

"They're always hungry," Hayley said happily. "I've started giving them a bowl of oatmeal in the mornings."

James stroked the head of the palest gray kitten. It rolled over and grasped his finger with playfully outstretched claws. "Ouch!" James laughed.

"Would Olive mind us visiting?" Mandy asked Hayley. "We've got something we'd like to show her."

Hayley hesitated. "Nana's very down today," she told them. "She's had some bad news." Then she smiled. "But she loves visitors, so I'll take you up. It might cheer her up a bit." She put the kitten back into the box and stood quickly. "I'll have to leave you with her, though. I've promised to help my mom in the kitchen."

"Maybe we shouldn't," James said.

"Don't worry. It'll be fine," Hayley assured him.

"OK," said Mandy, following her up the stairs.

They found Olive in her room, looking out at the peaceful scene below the window. The old lady had been crying. Her face was streaked with tears, and in her hand she held a crumpled handkerchief. She was looking through a pile of black-and-white photographs.

"Nana, it's Mandy and James. They've come to see you!" said Hayley. Then she made her way back downstairs.

Olive brightened a little when she recognized Mandy and James. "Sit down, and don't mind me," she said shakily. "I received a letter today that has upset me, that's all. How nice of you to come and see me again. Have you enjoyed your vacation?"

"Very much, thank you," Mandy smiled. "We've got something to show you." She nodded to James, who delved into the top pocket of his anorak. He handed the heavy silver watch to Olive.

Having reached for her glasses and put them on, the old lady studied it carefully. She opened the clasp and peered at the inscription inside. Then her hand trembled violently and flew to her mouth in sudden shock. "Where did you get this?" she said, breathlessly.

"On the moor . . ." Mandy began.

"But . . . *how* . . . after all this time?" Olive interrupted her. "This is William's watch. We gave it to him as a parting gift, the day he left to go to war." She kissed the watch and held it against her heart. "My dear, *dear* brother," she said.

Mandy looked at James. He was frowning deeply, his forehead crinkled behind his glasses. Mandy guessed he was trying to put together the pieces of the puzzle in his mind. "Will you tell us about your brother, Olive, please?" she asked softly.

"Oh, you're very kind, but I don't want to bore you young people with tales about the past." Olive smiled and sighed. "It was a long time ago."

"We'd like to hear about him," James said. "We really would."

"We grew up in a cottage on the moor," Olive began and her eyes glazed over as the memories came flooding back.

Mandy moved closer. She didn't want to miss a single detail of the old woman's story.

"There were very few people living in Dalton in those days, and as children we had the moor to ourselves," Olive continued. "The heath was our playground — a wild, beautiful place to roam. We played some wonderful games, William and I!"

Then Olive's smile faded. It was replaced by a look of love and great sadness. "William was just seventeen when the Great War began," she said quietly. "He joined to fight for our country."

"Which war was that?" Mandy asked.

"It was the First World War," Olive told them. "It began in 1914 and finished in 1918. It broke my mother's heart to see him go, and mine. And it broke the heart of his pet dog, too."

James sat bolt upright. "Dog?" he repeated, earning a withering look from Mandy.

"What kind of dog was he, Olive?" Mandy probed. Her heart was thudding so loudly that she was sure everyone would hear it.

"A greyhound, I think," Olive remembered. "Long legs . . . he was a gorgeous dog. He adored my brother. William had found him wandering when he was a puppy. He called him . . . Rover."

Mandy and James looked quickly at each other.

"The dog and he were devoted friends," Olive went on. "But then William went away to fight. He traveled to France and, soon after, we heard that he had been badly wounded when a shell exploded near him."

"Oh, no!" Mandy said, horrified.

"He spent months in the hospital recovering, but he never regained his hearing. Then we lost touch with him altogether. He just seemed to vanish." Olive's voice grew fainter with the sad memory, and she dabbed her eyes with her lace handkerchief. She blinked back a sudden rush of tears and Mandy put her hand out to comfort her.

"Did you try to find him?" James asked Olive.

She nodded. "All the army could tell us was that he had been officially listed as 'missing.' That's the term, you know, when they're not yet sure if a soldier is alive — or dead."

"Oh, dear." James looked at the floor uncomfortably.

Then Olive lifted her chin and smiled. "But he *did* survive the war. He made his way to western France, where he married a girl named Simone."

"But," Mandy frowned, "why didn't he come home to you, and the cottage on the moor and . . . Rover?"

"Because his memory was gone," Olive explained. "He had absolutely no recollection of us at all. It was the shock of the shelling, and his terrible wound, the horror of all he had seen. He just blanked it out. It was as if we had never existed."

"That's so sad," James said.

"But . . ." Mandy was struggling to make the puzzle fit, "if he didn't know about you, then how do *you* know about Simone, and about William being in France and everything?"

"Well, just yesterday I received a letter from Simone. William died last week, in his sleep. But, in the letter, she told me how William, a few hours before he died, had suddenly regained his memory. It had all come flooding back to him, and he told Simone about my mother and father, and me, and about our little flint-

and-thatch cottage on Dalton Heath. And, of course, about his beloved dog, Rover."

Mandy looked at James, her eyes huge with triumph and excitement.

"You see" — a shadow of sadness crossed Olive's face — "poor Rover died soon after William had left to go off to war," she whispered. "The memory of it haunts me still."

"How?" Mandy asked gently. "How did he die?"

"He refused to eat," Olive remembered. "He pined terribly for William. He sat at the front door day after day, waiting for his master to return. There was nothing we could do for him. He died of a broken heart."

"Oh, *poor* Rover!" Mandy's eyes filled with tears.

"I believe," Olive leaned forward and dropped her voice to a whisper, "that it is Rover who howls on the moor at night. He is still waiting for William to come home. . . ." She trailed off, and Mandy felt a shiver run the length of her spine. James's mouth gaped open. He blinked at Mandy.

"But maybe not," Olive sat up straight in her chair and took Mandy's hand. She squeezed it gently. "Perhaps that's just the foolish imagination of an old lady!"

"I don't think so," Mandy said softly. "I think you might be right."

"How kind you are," Olive said. "And to bring me this watch on today of all days! William dropped in to see us, the day he left to go to war. It was our parting gift to him."

"Mrs. Roberts," James ventured. "Where was your cottage?"

"I'm afraid that it burned to the ground some years ago. I am told just a pile of rubble remains to mark the place on the heath where it once stood."

Olive polished the pocket watch on the hem of her shawl. Then she kissed it gently and smiled. "Dear William," she whispered. "Rest in peace."

"Oh, I'm sure he will, Mrs. Roberts." Mandy smiled.

"Yes," James nodded. "He will. That's for sure."

Blackie sat with his head out of the window of the car. The wind whipped at his ears and his pink tongue lolled happily. "Well," said James, "I can't say that Blackie enjoyed camping."

Dr. Emily laughed. "He seems fine now."

"Perhaps he thought that all sorts of creepy creatures were out to get him on the moor," said Mandy mischievously. "Ghosts and things . . ."

"Don't be silly, Mandy," Dr. Emily said. Then she added, "Speaking of creepy things, we never did find out about the legend of the moor, did we? Remember the story in the guidebook about the brokenhearted dog?"

"Yes," Mandy replied absently. "I remember." She grinned at James and lowered her voice. "But something tells me that he won't be doing any more howling."

Mandy shifted in her seat, as something sharp dug into her leg. She reached into her pocket and pulled out the book that Mr. Moon had given to her.

"Look, James," she smiled, and together they flipped through the pages, looking at photographs of Dalton during the last hundred years.

Suddenly, Mandy and James froze as the book fell open at a very old photograph. They looked at each other.

The photograph showed William Johnston crouching down beside a beautiful greyhound. William was smiling broadly as Rover licked his face.

Mandy shook as a shiver ran through her. Then she smiled. "They're happy now," she said to James — and he grinned, too.

Then they settled back for the ride home to Welford.

HAUNTINGS

Look for the next spooky
Animal Ark™ Hauntings title:

WOLF AT THE WINDOW

"It's sort of sad, isn't it?" said Mandy as they walked past the main house and turned down the path. "To think that whole species of animals disappeared from this area before we even had a chance to see the animals in the wild."

"That's why wildlife parks are important," said James.

Dusk was just falling when they emerged from the woods and saw the lights of the lodge. Mandy realized that they'd missed lunch completely. Oatmeal *must* be filling.

Later that evening, after a meal of vegetarian chili

and salad, they sat by the fire in the living room. Blackie kept well out of the reach of the sparks.

"I meant to tell you, while I was getting dinner ready, I heard a news item about the young wolves at the wildlife park," Dr. Emily said.

Mandy and James sat up quickly.

"What did it say?" Mandy asked urgently. "I can't believe that I missed it!"

"It's all right, Mandy. I listened very carefully." Dr. Emily gave her a knowing smile. "I knew you'd want to hear all about it. Apparently, the wolves are captive-bred juveniles, less than two years old. They're from different packs — the hope is that eventually they will breed."

"Great," Mandy said.

"That's the good news, Mandy," her mom said. "The bad news is that the local farmers and ranchers are campaigning against them."

"But it's so wrong!" Mandy started to say more, but Dr. Emily shook her head.

"They have a right to their point of view, Mandy," she said. "They do have their livelihoods to worry about. They're worried that the wolves might escape and start killing their livestock."

"But we read up about wolves this afternoon. Hundreds of years ago, before people started killing lots of them, wolves used to keep the deer herds under control naturally," Mandy explained.

"But things were quite different then," Dr. Emily said. Then she softened. "I certainly don't agree with the farmers. They want to get rid of them any way they can."

Mandy was horrified. "What could they do?" she asked urgently.

"I hope they're not talking about using traps," Dr. Adam said from the depths of an armchair. "Those contraptions are positively barbaric. And illegal as well."

Mandy clenched her fists. She could feel anger welling up inside her as she remembered the trap that she'd read about in the library book. She slipped off her shoes, drew her feet up onto the chair, and sat hugging her knees. In the background, she could hear her parents and James talking, but she couldn't stop thinking about the young wolves' predicament.

Suddenly, Mandy began to feel uncomfortable. It was as if someone were watching her. Glancing around the room, her gaze was drawn to the window. Mandy felt her body go rigid and held her breath. It was there! The wolf was there! It was staring right at her.

This time, it couldn't possibly be her imagination. The wolf was enormous — Mandy could see its great mane of white fur shining in the moonlight. And its gaze was so intense that it seemed to bore right into her. She stared back at the wolf, not daring to look away for an instant, in case it disappeared.

"Mandy!" She could hear her mom calling her. Mandy didn't want to move, even to nod her head.

"Dad's suggesting we go to the wildlife park tomorrow," Dr. Emily said, then laughed. "Would you like to go, or is that a silly question?"

Mandy knew she had to respond. For a second, she dragged her gaze away from the sad yellow eyes of the great wolf to nod agreement to her mom.

But when she looked back, the wolf was gone.